Something was going on.

Lila's silver Subaru was parked in its usual spot in the concrete driveway. But it was far too early for her to be arriving home from work. James gave up the pretense of painting and watched as she got out of the car.

She was tall and curvy and had long blond curls that no amount of hair spray could tame. Lila had the body of a pinup girl and the brains of an accountant, a lethal combo. Then came his second clue that things were out of kilter. Lila was wearing jeans and a windbreaker. On a Monday.

He could have ignored all of that. Honestly, he was fine with the status quo. Lila had her job as vice president of the local bank, and James had the pleasure of dating women who were uncomplicated.

As he watched, Lila closed the driver's door and opened the passenger door. Leaning in, she gave him tantalizing view of a nicely rounded behind. He'd vays had a thing for butts. Lila's was first-class.

ıddenly, all thoughts of butts and sex and his long-;o love affair with his frustrating neighbor flew out e window.

ecause when Lila straightened, she was holding a ıby.

* * *

For Baby's Sake
is part of Mills & Boon Desire's
N⁰1 bestselling series, Billionaires and Babies:
Powerful men…wrapped around their babies' little fingers.

FOR BABY'S SAKE

BY
JANICE MAYNARD

First Published in Great Britain 2016
By Mills & Boon, an imprint of HarperCollins*Publishers*
1 London Bridge Street, London, SE1 9GF

© 2016 Janice Maynard

ISBN: 978-0-263-06517-6

Our policy is to use papers that are natural, renewable and recyclable
products and made from wood grown in sustainable forests. The logging
and manufacturing processes conform to the legal environmental
regulations of the country of origin.

Printed and bound in Great Britain
by CPI Antony Rowe, Chippenham, Wiltshire

USA TODAY bestselling author **Janice Maynard** loved books and writing even as a child. But it took multiple rejections before she sold her first manuscript. Since 2002, she has written over thirty-five books and novellas. Janice lives in east Tennessee with her husband, Charles. They love hiking, travelling and spending time with family.

You can connect with Janice at
www.Twitter.com/janicemaynard,
www.Facebook.com/janicemaynardreaderpage,
www.Wattpad.com/user/janicemaynard,
and www.Instagram.com/janicemaynard.

For Stacy Boyd, editor extraordinaire! She has been with the Kavanaghs from the beginning and loves them (almost) as much as I do. ☺ Stacy juggles a beautiful family and a demanding career with grace and professionalism. Here's to many more books together.

One

James Kavanagh liked working with his hands. Unlike his oldest brother, Liam, who spent his days wearing an Italian tailored suit, James was most comfortable in old jeans and T-shirts. Truth be told, it was a good disguise. No one expected a rich man to look like a guy who labored for a paycheck.

That was fine with James. He didn't need people sucking up to him because he was a Kavanagh. He wanted to be judged on his own merits. Sure, he was entitled to a share of the family fortune. And yes, he'd added to that considerable pot with his own endeavors.

But at the end of the day, a man was only as rich as his reputation.

At the moment, James was painting the soffits on his own house in the heart of Silver Glen, North Carolina. The 1920s bungalow was a beauty; original hardwood floors, large windows that let in plenty of light and a front porch that was made for enjoying warm summer evenings.

Of course, summer was little more than a memory now.

Before long, it would be time to put up the Christmas lights. When he'd thought about tackling that chore, he realized he had some peeling paint that needed attention. Such was the life of a carpenter. He poured most of his man-hours into renovating other people's homes. His own place came way down the list.

As he dipped his paintbrush in the can balanced precariously on the top of the ladder, something disturbed his concentration. Out of the corner of his eye, he saw movement at the house next door. Lila's house. A house he once knew all too well.

It didn't matter. He was over her. Completely. The two of them had been a fire that burned hot and bright, leaving only ashes. It was for the best. Lila was too uptight, too driven, too everything.

Still, something was going on. Lila's silver Subaru was parked in its usual spot in the concrete driveway. But it was far too early for her to be arriving home from work. He gave up the pretense of painting and watched as she got out of the car.

She was tall and curvy and had long blond curls that no amount of hair spray could tame. Lila had the body of a pinup girl and the brains of an accountant—a lethal combo. Then came his second clue that things were out of kilter. Lila was wearing jeans and a Windbreaker. On a Monday.

He could have ignored all of that. Honestly, he was fine with the status quo. Lila had her job as vice president of the local bank, and James had the pleasure of dating women who were uncomplicated. Not bimbos. He had his standards, after all. There was nothing wrong, though, with a guy having fun.

Did it matter if his most recent girlfriend thought Kazakhstan was a new heavy metal band? Not every woman had to be a rocket scientist.

As he watched, Lila closed the driver's door and opened the door to the backseat. Leaning in, she gave him a tantalizing view of a nicely rounded ass. He'd always had a thing for butts. Lila's was first-class.

Suddenly, all thoughts of butts and sex and his long-ago love affair with his frustrating neighbor flew out the window. Because when Lila straightened, she was holding a baby.

Lila had a blistering headache. It didn't help that James Kavanagh was watching her every move. He didn't even try to hide his interest. Sometimes she thought he deliberately worked outside so she could see his gorgeous body and obsess about everything she had lost.

Today she didn't care. Today she was in deep doo-doo. The humor in that comparison barely even registered.

Grabbing Sybbie's little body in a death grip so the squirmy infant wouldn't slide though her arms, Lila marched across the yard. At the base of James's ladder, she paused and stared up at him. "I need help," she said bluntly. "Will you come down so we can talk?"

If he agreed, it would be the first time in almost three years that the two of them had carried on more of a conversation than "nice day" or "your mail's on the porch." They tolerated each other. Politely. Which was not an easy thing to do when you had seen a man naked.

She closed that door firmly. "James?"

He appeared to be frozen. Suddenly, he dropped his paintbrush in the bucket and wiped his hands. "Of course."

As he descended the ladder, she was forced to back up. James was a big guy. Not fat. Oh, no. Not an ounce of spare flab anywhere on his six-foot-three-inch body. His brothers called him the gentle giant. It was an apt description.

James had the physique of a man who could break boulders with his bare hands. Muscular, broad-shouldered and impressively strong, he was a man's man. He also happened to be incredibly tender when making love to a woman who was half his size, but that was information from another time, another place, another Lila.

He stared at the baby, his expression inscrutable. "What's up, Lila? Who's this little charmer?" His thick, wavy, chestnut hair was overdue for a trim.

"Her name is Sybbie. My half sister died. She and her boyfriend. In a car accident." It was still difficult to talk about, still impossible to believe.

"God, honey. I'm so sorry."

She swallowed hard, almost undone by the genuine sympathy and concern in his rich brown eyes and deep voice. "I hadn't seen her in a decade. She didn't like me very much. But for some reason, she named me in her will as the baby's guardian. Sybbie is almost eight months old."

James's intense scrutiny made her nervous. "And you accepted?"

"I didn't have much of a choice in the short term. There may be other options. But for now, I have her."

"I see." She felt his doubt almost tangibly. James knew her feelings about children. It was part of the reason they had split up. "So, why do you need to talk to me?"

"My house needs some modifications."

"For a short-term situation?"

"I am a responsible adult. I won't endanger a baby simply because it inconveniences me. My bedroom is on the top floor. I want to turn the dining room into a nursery, and I'll move into the downstairs bedroom."

"Makes sense."

His grudging approval eased some of the tightness in her chest. "Do you have time in your schedule to do what needs to be done?" James bought houses and flipped them. His work was meticulous. Many of the finest homes in the historic district had been restored by James.

"I'll have to juggle some things, but I think I can make it work. Who's going to keep the kid?"

It was a fair question and an obvious one. The only fully licensed child care center in Silver Glen took babies when they were twelve months or older. "I've used my paid time off for bereavement and more than a week of my two-week vacation, counting today. But I have four days left."

"Four days? What about maternity leave?" His raised eyebrow made her feel guilty for no good reason.

"That will only kick in if I actually adopt Sybbie. The auditors will be here next Monday. I can't miss that. I'll figure out something."

James stared at her. She refused to fidget. Working in the upper echelons of a profession traditionally dominated by men had taught her to look unshakeable even when she was nervous on the inside.

When he still didn't speak, she snapped at him. "What?"

James's shoulders lifted and fell in a deep sigh. "Caring for an eight-month-old is a lot of work." He wasn't merely tossing out platitudes. All six of his brothers were married, and most of them had kids. The youngest Kavanagh sibling was a beloved uncle. She had seen that with her own two eyes…a hundred years ago when she had been James's girlfriend for a tempestuous three months.

He was right to have doubts about her. But at the moment, she didn't see any other options. "I know that," she said quietly, refusing to be hurt by his unspoken assessment of her nurturing talents. "I'm not afraid of hard work. Will you come next door with me and let me show you what I'm thinking?"

"Sure."

He strode beside her as they crossed from his hand-kerchief-sized lawn to hers. The next embarrassing moment was not being able to unlock the front door while holding the baby.

James took the little girl without asking. At last the stupid key turned and they were able to go inside. The house hadn't changed at all since the last time James was here. But he didn't utter a single comment to make her uncomfortable. An observer would have noticed nothing in his demeanor to suggest that he and Lila had once made love leaning over the sturdy, oak dining room table.

Her cheeks heated. "Through here," she muttered.

Sybbie seemed enamored with the new man in her life. She was a quiet, easy child, her temperament sunny unless she was tired or hungry.

Lila stopped in the kitchen doorway. "I don't really need a dining room, anyway. I never use it. After Sybbie is gone, the nursery could always be turned into a small den or a sitting room for the guest room."

James rubbed the baby's downy head. She had hair that was white-blond, her pink cheeks completing the look of a chubby angel. "How long will that be, Lila? Do you even know?"

"I told you. I'm not sure." And there was the rub. Because for Lila to function at maximum capacity, she *really* needed to be sure. About everything. Uncertainty drove her nuts. Since the moment she'd received the heart-wrenching phone call about her sister's death, life had been nothing *but* uncertainty.

James took a step away, allowing her to breathe normally. He examined load-bearing walls, scribbled a few measurements on a scrap of paper and paced off the dimensions of the dining room. All the while holding the baby as if it were the most natural thing in the world.

At last, he turned. "Shouldn't be a problem. But you and Sybbie will need to move over to my place for a couple of nights. When I'm sledgehammering walls, it won't be safe for you or the baby to breathe the air."

"What about you?"

"I wear a mask when I'm doing demolition."

"I'm sure I could go to a hotel for a few nights." The thought of sleeping under James's roof again gave her hives.

His scowl told her in no uncertain terms what he thought of the hotel idea. That had been one of their problems actually. James had a maddening habit of telling people what to do. The two of them had butted heads over the issue time and again.

"Be reasonable, Lila," he said, clearly trying for a conciliatory tone. "A hotel is no place for a baby. I have a refrigerator for formula and everything you could possibly need, save a baby bed. But you were going to have to buy that, anyway."

What he said made perfect sense. But she wouldn't. She couldn't. "James, um…well, considering our past… it would be—"

He held up his hand, his expression grim. "Let me stop you right there. The past is the past, Lila. You and I were a bad match from the beginning. But we both know that now. You're a neighbor and a friend. That's all. What happened three years ago has nothing to do with this."

Her stomach curled. That was easy for him to say. James had moved on. And he hadn't wasted any time. She'd seen him with a parade of women, each one more beautiful than the last. It wasn't James's feelings she was worried about. It was her own.

James Kavanagh had no interest in bedding her again. That was clear. But she still had feelings for him, even if most of those feelings were hormones. It would be incredibly foolhardy to put herself in his path. She had Sybbie to think of now. She couldn't afford more heartbreak.

The trouble was, she was fresh out of options. James's suggestion made perfect sense. But she didn't have to like it. "Fine," she said, trying not to sound huffy. "We'll take you up on your kind invitation."

His nod was terse. "Not tonight. I have a project I promised to finish up in the morning. But I'll help you move tomorrow evening. You can have the baby bed delivered to my house."

"James Kavanagh. You know I can't do that. Gossip spreads faster than kudzu around here."

He shrugged. "So what? I think my reputation can handle it. Are you worried about your fancy bank job?"

His smart-ass tone made her see red. "You always hated my job, didn't you?"

He leaned against the door frame, his dark-eyed gaze unreadable. "I never hated the job, Lila. I merely hated the fact that it consumed you. There's more to life than work."

"Says the man with a trust fund. Some of us need a little security."

The sudden silence mushroomed between them. Here they were, three full years after the nuclear detonation of their relationship, still fighting the same tired battle.

James shook his head. "I didn't mean to go there. I'm sorry."

"Me, either. Maybe this will work better if we pretend we've only known each other a few weeks."

He chuckled. "I don't think I'm that good of an actor, but I'll try. What if you order the baby bed tomorrow morning, and I'll pick it up after work?"

"And tonight?"

"You can keep her upstairs with you for one night. You have a king-size bed...right?"

"Yes." He knew full well that she did, damn it. They had certainly made use of the big mattress and the spindled headboard.

"Put Sybbie in with you and tuck the covers as tightly

as you can under the mattress. That way she won't be able to roll out."

"Okay. You're right. That will be fine."

He shifted from one foot to the other. Sybbie was almost asleep, her tiny eyelids drooping. "Is that all?" James asked. "I need to get back to work."

Lila flushed. She had asked him to treat her like a virtual stranger. But she hadn't expected it to hurt so much. "Of course," she said brightly. "Let me take her from you."

James seemed almost reluctant to give up the little girl. Maybe he thought Lila wasn't capable of being a competent caregiver. When the baby passed from him to her, James's fingers brushed Lila's breasts. It was a simple contact. Unavoidable. Fleeting at best.

Even so, her body's instinctive reaction told her the next few weeks were going to be a challenge. She'd gotten over James Kavanagh once. She didn't have it in her to do it again.

Two

James got out of bed, thirsty, at 3:00 a.m. As he stood in the bathroom and downed a glass of water, it was impossible to ignore the fact that a light burned in Lila's upstairs bedroom window. Hell. The baby must be awake.

It wasn't any of his business. It wasn't his concern.

He could give himself all the lectures in the world, but it wasn't going to change the facts. Lila was in trouble, and he needed to fix things.

Wasn't this the theme of one of their many fights? She was a grown woman who wanted to take care of herself.

But tonight was different. Being a new parent was hard and scary for almost everyone. Especially a woman with a kid who wasn't even her own...a child who had been thrust willy-nilly into the middle of Lila's perfectly manicured life.

Cursing beneath his breath, he pulled on a pair of pants and shoved his feet into leather slippers. It was in the thirties outside. He found a clean button-up shirt and threw his leather jacket on over it.

Then he stopped, stymied by how to get past this next hurdle. If he rang the doorbell at this ungodly hour, he might scare Lila to death. Even worse, if the baby was finally on the verge of sleep. Lila would string him up by his toes if he woke little Sybbie.

There really was only one logical choice. He pulled out his cell phone and scrolled through his contacts. He didn't want to admit he still had Lila's phone number. It wasn't a thing. He'd just never gotten around to deleting it.

Quickly, he typed a text:

I see your light on. Would you like me to come hold the baby so you can sleep for a few hours? I was up anyway.

He leaned against the wall beside the window, looking for a reaction. Nothing happened. It was possible that Lila had left her phone downstairs. Or maybe it was turned off. Damn.

Suddenly, his phone dinged.

Yes! Please. I suck at this.

He laughed out loud. That was one thing he'd always loved about Lila, her sense of humor. He ran down the stairs and out the side door, oddly unconcerned that it was the middle of the night. He didn't require a lot of sleep, anyway. Helping out with little Sybbie wouldn't be a hardship.

On Lila's porch, he paused, but she was at the door ready to let him in. When he saw her, he had to hold back a chuckle. She was undeniably disheveled. She had tried to put her hair up in a ponytail, but the baby must have grabbed it, because one whole side was falling down.

On her T-shirt he saw what might have been a mixture

of baby food and drool. He cocked his head and smiled. "Tough day at the office, dear?"

Lila bristled. "Don't make fun of me, James Buchanan Kavanagh. I might have to shoot you in cold blood, and then what would poor Sybbie do? Her aunt in prison and her only babysitter deader than dead."

He raised his hands in the universal sign of surrender. "Message received. Show me where the cable remote is and go to bed. Little Princess and I will be fine."

Lila hesitated. "Seriously, James? This isn't your problem. You have to work tomorrow."

"So do you," he said firmly. "And it's a good bet that juggling Sybbie for twelve hours will be a heckuva lot harder than sitting behind your desk all day."

"Is that a criticism?" She was tired, but not too tired to give him grief.

"Only an observation." He took the baby from her. "I can find the remote on my own. Go. You're about to fall over."

Her gorgeous blue eyes filled with tears. "Thank you, James."

Lila was not the crying type. Tomorrow it would piss her off that he had seen her at such a vulnerable point. But there was nothing he could do about that. "It's not a big deal, Lila. Get some sleep."

The fact that she obeyed him without further protest told him she was at the end of her rope. This was only her first week as a mom. How was she going to manage?

Shaking off his disquiet, he concentrated on the little girl who nestled so trustingly in his arms. She was tired. Anybody could see that. Maybe it was the new surroundings that had her out of sorts. Poor kid wouldn't understand why her parents weren't around…or why she wasn't in her familiar bedroom.

"Come on, little Sybbie. Let's see what Aunt Lila has on late-night cable."

Seeing the soft, high-end leather sofa gave him a weird vibe. He and Lila had spent many a night cuddling on that particular piece of furniture. Nothing good would come of dwelling on those memories. It would only make him horny, and tonight he had better things to do than rehash old love affairs.

By the time he settled into the soft cushions, dimmed the lights and wrapped an afghan around the baby, little Sybbie was yawning. He rubbed her back and sang to her softly about small spiders and babies rocking in trees. She smelled good…like babies were supposed to smell.

He was struck by a bolt of sadness that made no sense. Everything in his life was going great. It was true he envied his brothers and their growing families, but he was young. He had plenty of time to find the kind of woman his siblings had found. Then it would be time for him to do the whole slippers-by-the-fire thing. Making sure Sybbie was secure against his chest, he yawned and closed his eyes. The baby was asleep already. He would catch a few z's before she woke up again. That's what all the baby experts said. Sleep when the baby sleeps…

Lila fell into bed and was dead to the world in seconds. An hour later, though, she sat straight up, her heart racing in a panicked rhythm. Sybbie. Where was she?

Everything came crashing back. The past day and night had been a challenge, but Lila had done everything she was supposed to do. Sybbie had eaten a good dinner of pears and sweet potatoes, Gerber style. Then, she had seemed perfectly happy and normal when Lila got out a collection of small metal pots and pans and colorful plastic containers. She even laughed when Lila built towers on the rug and helped Sybbie knock them down.

Nothing out of the ordinary had occurred until Lila tried to give the baby her bedtime bottle. Lila had researched the appropriate formulas and amounts. Carefully, she tested the temperature on her wrist to make sure it was exactly right. Sybbie responded with a happy gurgle.

What was supposed to happen next was that the baby went to sleep until morning. Unfortunately, Sybbie hadn't read the same baby manuals. She finished her bottle and wanted to play again. That lasted until midnight, at which point she threw a baby-sized tantrum.

It wasn't the little one's fault. Poor sweetheart had had her life turned upside down. Knowing the cause, though, didn't help when Lila's body craved sleep. Getting James's text was a lifesaver. She probably shouldn't have accepted his offer so quickly, but she had been almost comatose.

Now she'd had just enough of a snooze that her adrenaline was flowing again. The house was quiet. Too quiet.

Carefully, she crept down the stairs, avoiding the ones that squeaked. If Sybbie was asleep, she dared not wake her up.

The scene in the living room took her heart and gave it a good hard twist, almost a physical pain. The lights were low. The TV was on, but the sound was muted. James was stretched out with his feet propped on the coffee table. Sybbie slept blissfully on James's chest, her knees tucked under her and her little bottom up in the air.

The afghan had fallen to the floor, but neither man nor baby seemed to care.

What should she do now? With the hour of good, solid sleep she'd had, surely she could take over and let James go home. But it seemed a shame to wake him. Not only that, if they disturbed the baby, all of James's efforts would have been in vain.

Lila yawned. According to the mantel clock, it was still a good two hours before the sun would come up. She might as well join them. Grabbing the afghan off the floor, she covered her two guests and found a blanket of her own. She curled up in the recliner and closed her eyes.

James groaned, trying to figure out why his back ached and why the dog was sitting on his chest. He opened his eyes and blinked. The world came into focus slowly. It was eight o'clock in the morning, and his charge still slept peacefully. He needed to hit the john, but he didn't want to disturb the child.

Across the room, Lila was a lump in the recliner, the top of her head barely visible above the edge of her blanket. He smiled in spite of his physical discomfort. She must have come downstairs at some point and not wanted to wake him.

Evidently, he made a noise in spite of himself, because she jerked straight up in the chair and stared around the room wild-eyed.

He waved a hand to get her attention. "Everything is fine," he whispered. "The baby's still sleeping."

Lila stood up and stretched, giving him a mouthwatering view of her flat belly and cute navel. "Thank God for that," she muttered. Then she frowned at him. "Why are you still here? You have to go to work."

Her tone irritated him. "You might try saying, 'Thank you, James.' 'You saved my butt, James.'"

"Sorry," she muttered. "I do appreciate it." She sounded like a little kid being forced to thank Grandma for an ugly Christmas sweater.

Their entire conversation was being conducted in whispers. Thankfully, Sybbie was sleeping so deeply now, she never stirred. She had missed out on several hours of slumber the night before. Clearly, she was making up for lost time.

Carefully, he stood up, his hand cradling the baby's

back. "If you'll take her, I'll go home and get ready for work. I wouldn't leave, but I promised Mrs. Bellamy that I'd finish stabilizing her banister and newel post this morning."

Lila was flushed, either from sleep or because she was flustered. "Of course you have to go."

They finessed the baby transfer without a hitch.

James rubbed the crick in his neck. "Can you manage ordering the baby bed?"

"Yes," Lila said, her voice curt. "I'm not totally incompetent."

"I never said you were."

They stared at each other across the room, the sofa between them. Old wounds had inexplicably opened up, leaving both of them on edge.

Lila sighed deeply. "I apologize, James, for being so touchy. It's the lack of sleep. I'm extremely grateful for everything you did last night."

He nodded. "I'll call you later. We'll come up with a plan."

Three

Lila had to fight the urge to beg. *Don't leave me. I can't do this. Please help me.* She swallowed the words and bit down on her lip until the door closed behind James. Then she sank into a chair and sighed. What was she supposed to do now? Maybe she could grab a little more sleep to get her through the afternoon and evening.

But no sooner had she sat down than Sybbie woke up, her blue eyes sunshiny with happiness. She reached up to pull Lila's earring. Lila intercepted the small fingers. "No, sweet thing. You're too young for that. Come on, baby girl. How do you feel about mango applesauce and toast?"

The day flew by, but inexplicably, Lila had nothing to show for it by five o'clock other than a hamper full of dirty clothes, a floor strewn with makeshift toys and a kitchen that looked like it had been ground zero for a nuclear explosion.

She *did* get online and order the crib and mattress and bedding, but only because she couldn't bear to see the look of smug superiority James would give her if she dropped the ball on that detail. The baby store was a local company in Silver Glen. They delivered the boxes to her front porch before the close of the business day. She'd texted James and told him he didn't need to pick them up. That had never been an option as far as she was concerned.

When he showed up at her door at five thirty, it would have been nice if she could have invited him in for a nice hot dinner…maybe wearing a cute top and a flirty above-the-knee skirt. Instead, he was about to see the disaster that was her day.

Balancing the baby on her hip, she shoved the hair from her face and opened the door. "Hey," she said. "Did you get everything done you needed to do?"

He nodded, but he looked tired. "Yep. How's my girl?"

Lila's heart skipped a beat until she realized the teasing affection was directed at the baby.

James took Sybbie and nuzzled her nose with his. "How's it hangin', sweetheart?"

The Kavanagh men, one and all, were handsome, virile and completely charming. An eight-month-old baby didn't stand a chance. Lila had spent an entire day playing the clown to keep her charge in a good mood. All James had to do was show up and the child was instantly mesmerized. Sigh…

"I was going to order takeout," Lila said. "Would you like me to get enough for two?"

James nodded. "Sounds good. I'm easy to please. After you make that call, why don't you gather what you and Sybbie need, and I'll start carrying everything over to my place. I've cleared out the downstairs bedroom."

Lila knew that the floor plan of James's house was similar to hers. But he had turned his traditional dining room into an office. For a couple of nights, it would work as a nursery. Still, she felt guilty.

"It's the off-season," she said. "I'm sure your mom would give me a room up at the hotel." The Silver Beeches Lodge was Silver Glen's premier accommodation, where the rich and famous went to get away from it all and have their privacy protected. Located on top of the mountain, it commanded a spectacular view of the valley below. It was owned by the Kavanagh family and managed by James's oldest brother, Liam, and his mother, Maeve Kavanagh.

"Of course she would. But it's not necessary, Lila. I'm right next door."

What he said made sense, but she was uneasy about the idea.

He saw her hesitation. His jaw firmed. "If you're worried about you and me, don't be. I won't do anything to make you uncomfortable, I swear."

Except be you. That was the tough part. She had learned to pretend James Kavanagh didn't exist. The subterfuge would be impossible to maintain now. "I know you won't," she said defensively. She didn't want him to think she was pining away for him.

"Okay, then. I'll take the baby bed over and put it together. Call me when the food gets here."

James wasn't stupid. He knew Lila didn't want his help, and he also knew she was antsy around him. Though they had ended their relationship long ago, the physical pull was still there. He sure as hell felt it.

If Lila had been faced with *any* crisis, he would have offered to assist, even if she turned him down. But in this instance, there was a baby involved. Lila might not want his help with her niece, but she was going to get it.

Knocking the crib together was no trouble at all. He barely even glanced at the instructions. He'd spent most of his adult life working with tools and lumber and varnish and paint. Maybe because he'd never known his father,

he'd always been drawn to pursuits that were traditionally masculine. As if he could somehow make up for his
male parent's absence.

The patriarch of the Kavanagh family was the stuff of
legend. James was the only brother who had no memory
of him at all, though even Patrick's recollections were
hazy. Reggie Kavanagh had become obsessed with finding the lost silver mine that launched the family fortunes
decades before.

Kavanagh wealth and influence had founded Silver
Glen. The small town with its alpine feel and cozy charm
drew visitors from all over the world. Careful planning
and restriction had kept overbuilding under control.

Sadly, Reggie Kavanagh gave his life in pursuit of a
pipe dream. He set out one day on yet another of his hunting expeditions—hunting for the lost mine—and never
returned. After several years, the coroner issued a death
certificate listing the deceased as "presumed dead," but
not knowing for sure had left its mark on each of the
Kavanaghs in different ways.

James stood and stretched his back. The bed looked
sturdy and shiny. He would let Lila deal with the sheets
and stuff. Women had ideas about that kind of thing.

He cleaned up the leftover bits and pieces and carried
the cardboard out to the recycle bin. It was dark now. The
lights shining from Lila's house cast a cozy glow across
the space that separated their homes. Sometimes he wondered if he and Lila could have done anything differently
to salvage their relationship. But in the end, he had con-
cluded that they were simply too different.

They wanted vastly divergent things out of life. The
gulf was so wide, neither of them had been able to see
any room for compromise.

James hated failing at anything. Growing up with six

brothers had honed his competitive instincts. But love wasn't a sport. Sex? Maybe. Love? Not at all.

In his pocket, his cell phone dinged. He pulled it out.

Pizza's here.

His stomach rumbled right on cue. Not bothering to lock his door, he loped across the side yard. He wasn't in love with Lila anymore. He probably never was. But he was curiously pleased about the thought of having her close at hand again.

Did that make him a sick, complicated bastard? Perhaps. Still, there were worse addictions. Lila's front door was unlocked, so he let himself in. Crime happened in Silver Glen, but it was rare. The community was tight-knit, and visitors tended to be movers and shakers who paid top dollar for lodging.

He found his two soon-to-be houseguests in Lila's kitchen. Apparently, Lila had ordered a high chair in addition to the bed. Sybbie seemed to be enjoying her new perch.

Lila shoved the box across the table. "Help yourself. I bought plenty."

It shouldn't have surprised him that she remembered his favorite toppings. Lila Baxter was a detail person... Type A to the max, but in a lot of good ways. She was organized and energetic, and she had a knack for juggling several projects at once. It wasn't her fault that life had tossed her the one ball she was likely to drop.

They ate quietly except for the baby's gurgles and coos. He could hear a clock ticking in the other room.

To anyone looking in the window, they would appear to be an ordinary American family. Appearances could be deceiving.

When he couldn't let the uncomfortable silence drag on

a moment more, he stood up abruptly. "Why don't I take Sybbie? That will make it easier for you to pack a bag."

Lila nodded, her eyes not quite meeting his. "Sounds good. Thanks."

James took the baby and left, his chest tight. At this rate, he and Lila were going to kill each other with politeness. It was a stupid, artificial situation. But the only alternatives he knew with her were hot, crazy sex and shouting matches. Neither of those was gonna fly right now, so kindness it was.

Four

Lila was still learning how to pack a diaper bag. The sheer amount of stuff a baby needed these days was incredible. She threw a few of her own things into a small carry-all and made one last sweep of the bedroom to be sure she hadn't forgotten anything.

Walking into James's house took all the courage she possessed. She paused in the foyer, hearing his footsteps upstairs and the rumble of his voice as he talked to the baby.

While man and child were occupied, she scoped out the new living arrangements. James had made amazing progress in such a short time frame. She knew he had a habit of using his spare bedroom for a dumping ground. But all the sports equipment and miscellany had been cleared away. The queen bed was neatly made and the small attached bathroom was spotless.

In the office, James had moved things out of the way to accommodate the crib. Lila put a sheet on the small mattress and smoothed the wrinkles from the soft cotton that was printed with gamboling monkeys and bananas. Already, she had decided not to shroud little Sybbie in everything pink. This was the twenty-first century. Her niece might grow up to be president one day.

James and Sybbie found her just as she was finishing up. She wrinkled her nose. "I think I read somewhere that you're supposed to wash baby things before you use them the first time. But I don't want to delay her bedtime."

"It won't matter for just one night. You can do a load of laundry tomorrow."

"Okay." Wow. This was never going to work if they couldn't loosen up. The tension headache had started as soon as she walked into his house.

James's phone dinged, signaling a text. When he pulled it out and looked at it, his face reddened.

"What's wrong?" she asked, faintly alarmed by the look of consternation on his face.

"Nothing. Nothing at all. But I have a date tonight and I need to hit the road."

She gaped at him before snapping her mouth shut and straightening her spine. "I'll take Sybbie. Have fun." The words felt like sandpaper in her throat. She took the baby from him, careful not to let her hands brush his.

"We'll try not to disturb you when we come in."

We? Lila felt the color drain from her cheeks. Her stomach felt funny…as if she had swallowed bad milk. "No problem. I'll close our doors. You won't bother us at all."

James strode out of his own house like a felon fleeing the scene of a crime. He jumped in his car, turned the ignition hard enough to bend the key and peeled out of the driveway with a squeal of tires. Hell, hell, hell. Why had he ever suggested this asinine arrangement?

He'd completely forgotten he had a date with a beautiful woman tonight. A woman who had given strong hints that she was up for any kind of recreation he had in mind. There was absolutely no reason in the world for him to feel guilty about his social calendar.

Then why did the memory of Lila's stricken expression make him feel like a complete ass?

During dinner and a movie, he told himself to forget about Sybbie and Lila. He'd offered them a temporary home while he knocked out a wall. No big deal.

Even though his companion for the evening was sweet and smart and probably nicer than he deserved, he could barely keep up with the conversation over drinks at his brother's watering hole, The Silver Dollar Saloon. Fortunately, Dylan wasn't in residence. James wasn't in the mood to be razzed about anything, much less his attractive date.

Somehow, he felt as if he had cheated on *two* women, but the truth was, he hadn't done anything dishonest at all. His righteous indignation prompted him to ask his date in for coffee. At his house.

But after two cups of decaf, when she made it clear she expected to be escorted upstairs, he created some lame excuse about having to get up early and took her home.

By the time he made it back, it was late. Late enough that Lila was probably, hopefully, asleep. He was cranky and horny and tired. And now he had to tiptoe around his own house.

He let himself in quietly and took his shoes off at the front door. Since he'd moved in half a dozen years ago, he had put a lot of TLC into the little house. Now there wasn't a single stair that creaked, which hopefully meant he wouldn't disturb his houseguest when he went up to his room.

Unfortunately, he wasn't ready to go to sleep yet. He was wired. Maybe he could grab a beer and watch some TV with the sound turned down so as not to bother anybody. It was a good plan until he pushed open the swinging door to the kitchen and flipped on the light, practically mowing down Lila in the process and causing her to drop a glass of milk that shattered all over the floor.

"Good Lord." He grabbed her arms to steady her. She was wearing a tank top and pajama pants, leaving her shoulders bare. He had forgotten how soft her skin was, how fragile her bones.

Lila jerked away from him, her eyes huge, her pupils dilated. "I'm sorry. I couldn't sleep. I wanted something to drink."

"Don't move. You'll cut yourself." Her feet were bare. He picked her up by the waist and set her on the counter. "Let me get this mess cleaned up."

He felt Lila's gaze on him as he grabbed a broom and a wet rag to deal with the floor. But she didn't say a word. He was glad. There wasn't a knife big enough to cut the tension in the room.

When he finished his task, he straightened and stared at her. "I owe you an apology," he said gruffly.

"For what?"

"What I said earlier about being quiet when we came in. It was a cheap shot. In a battle you and I aren't even fighting anymore."

"So you didn't sleep with her?"

James was pretty sure she didn't mean to blurt that out. "No. I didn't. We only just met."

"That's never stopped you before."

He sucked in a breath and watched Lila's face turn red. This was why things were always going to be like a minefield between the two of them. The memories were combustible. Lila had moved into her new house on a Monday almost three and a half years ago. James had gone over to meet the new neighbor and offer his assistance. Two weeks later they were in bed together.

"Let's not get sidetracked," he said, wishing his throat wasn't so damn dry. "I was trying to apologize."

"Then why did you do it?"

Why, indeed? Lila's blue eyes judged him and found him guilty…or so it seemed. He shrugged. "I didn't want you to get any ideas. Or to think that my invitation was something more than it was."

Her small smile was wry. "I didn't. Believe me. We were pretty dreadful together. I don't want to go through that again."

"Not all of it was so terrible." He saw in her eyes that she remembered the same things he did. The incredible sexual chemistry that made them crazy for each other.

"No," she said quietly. "It wasn't all bad. But we're too smart to go down that road again. Aren't we?"

That was the million-dollar question. Three years ago they had fought incessantly, almost from the beginning. He resented her crazy hours. She was angry that he didn't understand her need to prove herself and pursue a promotion. James wanted to start a family before he turned thirty. Lila didn't think she wanted to have children at all.

In the end, all the fabulous sex in the world couldn't disguise the fact that they were oil and water. And both hardheaded, to boot.

After a few beats of silence, he cleared his throat. "Did the baby have any trouble going to sleep?"

Lila pulled her knees to her chest and linked her arms around her legs. "No, thank goodness. I actually called Mia for advice. She told me I should put Sybbie down awake and let her coo and squirm until she put herself to sleep. It worked. I couldn't believe it, but it worked."

Mia was James's sister-in-law… Dylan's wife. She and Lila had become friends three years ago, and fortunately, the friendship had survived James and Lila's breakup.

It was no wonder the two women had bonded. They were both extremely smart and ambitious.

"You look tired," he said impulsively.

"Another cheap shot?" Her expression was equal parts wary and defensive.

"Not at all. I suppose that was my way of saying I'm worried about you. This whole situation with your sister's death can't have been easy, even if you *were* estranged. You never told me much about your family when you and I were dating."

It was Lila's turn to shrug. "Not much to tell. My dad walked out when I was three. My mother married again and got pregnant right away. But she was a functioning alcoholic and my new stepfather was a recreational drug user, so we lived close to the poverty line. My half sister, Alicia, followed their example."

"I'm sorry."

"Alicia and I struggled through the typical sibling rivalries, but as we got older, I did well in school, and she didn't. I think she may have had a learning disability."

"So you had a way out of a bad situation, and she didn't."

"Yes. I've always wondered if I could have done more to help her."

"People make their own choices, good or bad."

"I know. Still, it made me sad."

"And you didn't know she had named you as Sybbie's guardian?"

"Not a clue. I was completely shocked."

"My guess is that she knew you were smart and successful and that she could trust you with the baby."

"Maybe. Or I could have been the lesser of two evils. My mother is still living, but she has multiple health issues. She wouldn't be able to handle a small child at her age and in her condition. My brother-in-law grew up in foster homes, so there's no one on that side of the family."

"Which leaves you."

"Yes."

"You can't be legally compelled by a will you knew nothing about."

"I know. My lawyer made that clear. But how can I let her go to foster care and the adoptive system? How would I live with myself?"

"There's time to think about it. You can't solve everything in one night."

When Lila tried to hop down from the counter, he stopped her. "I may not have gotten all the glass. Hold still." He took her by the waist again, swung her over the sticky area and set her in the doorway. "Do you want me to get you another glass of milk?"

Lila shook her head. "No. I'm good. I'll see you in the morning."

"I have a housekeeper who comes in at ten. I've told her to avoid the guest room and my office for the time being."

"I'm inconveniencing you. Why won't you let me go to a hotel?"

"I think I owe you one." He hadn't meant to be so honest. Something about her demeanor tonight sneaked past his defenses.

She wrapped her arms around her waist. "You don't owe me anything, James. Really. We both made mistakes. And it was a long time ago."

"Okay. Fair enough. But quit worrying about everything so much. You'll be back in your own house before you know it."

Five

As it turned out, James's prediction was wildly optimistic. The day after the milk incident, she barely saw him at all other than the times she peeked out the window and watched him going in and out of her house. He had ordered a Dumpster and had it delivered right outside. It was slowly filling with chunks of Sheetrock and pieces of wallpaper.

He had told Lila she and Sybbie would have to be displaced only two nights, but at dinner that first night—lasagna prepared by his wonderful housekeeper before she left—he sat down at the table and ran a hand through his hair, his expression agitated.

"What's wrong, James?" He'd never been good at hiding his feelings. "Is it going to take longer than you thought?"

He rubbed his chin and shook his head. "I might have run into a bit of a snag today."

Sybbie didn't like having Lila's attention elsewhere. She wailed until Lila gave her another bite of bread. "Go ahead and tell me," Lila said. "I can handle bad news."

"You have termites."

She blinked at him. "Say that again?"

"Termites."

"But I have a pest control service."

"That's a good thing, because they'll have to repair the damage at their own expense. You still have termites, though. I can't work on the renovation until we take care of that."

Her throat got tight and her eyes burned. She was trying so hard to stay positive, but this was a kick in the stomach. "What do I need to do?"

His gaze softened. "*You* don't have to do anything, Lila, except take care of this little sweetheart." He tickled Sybbie's neck and was rewarded with a smile. "I'll handle your house issues. I've seen worse."

"I can't let you do that."

"Too late." His grin blinded her. "You've already hired me."

"To do a modest renovation, not to rip out all my walls."

"Don't be a drama queen."

She felt her temper rise and had to tamp it down. He was teasing her…that's all. An old habit. Perhaps the reason she and James had fought so much when they were together was because the making up afterward had been so much fun. But that wasn't going to happen this time around. Which meant she couldn't let him press her buttons.

"How long are we talking about?"

"If your termite people are on the ball, not long. They'll have to do a major treatment. The more pressing issue is whether or not you have termites anywhere else."

She hadn't even thought of that implication. "People told me not to buy an old house. I should have listened."

"Oh, come on, Lila. You know you love the place."

"I do. But I don't want it falling down around my ears."

Having an infant at the table made adult conversation

difficult. By unspoken consent, they tabled the termite talk and played with the baby. Wistfully, Lila watched James interact with Sybbie. Maeve Kavanagh had raised seven sons, mostly on her own. She had instilled in them the value of hard work and what it meant to be a gentleman.

To an outsider, the Kavanagh men might seem very different from one another. But under the skin—beneath the superficial differences of physical appearance and career choice—they each were carbon copies when it came to their character. Alpha males one and all. Tough, uncompromising. Committed to doing what was right even when the choice was difficult.

Hence her stint camping out in James's guest room.

"Tell me something," she said impulsively.

He looked up, his beautiful brown eyes regarding her with a hint of reserve. Maybe he thought she was going to give him grief about last night. "What is it? What do you want to know? I'm an open book."

That wasn't exactly true. He *seemed* like an open book, but she had a feeling she had only scratched the surface when it came to understanding James Kavanagh.

"Are you still looking for your father's remains?"

"Where the hell did that come from?" Anger flashed in his gaze, warning her to tread lightly. But surely this was the key. Something about a son without a father and James's insistence on having children. It wasn't the kind of thing most guys who were barely thirty fixated on.

She handed Sybbie a small bite of banana. "When you and I were together, you spent a lot of weekends out in the woods. Searching. And every time you came home, I got the feeling you were upset. But I was always afraid to ask you."

"Afraid? Of me?"

"I'm talking about your state of mind. When you came to pick me up for dates and you had been out on the mountain, I sensed a wildness in you, as if you were barely under control. Am I wrong?"

"I don't want to talk about my father." His tone said *back off.*

"I never knew my father either, James, not really. It's a sad way to grow up. But at least you have a fabulous mother...and all your siblings."

"If you think I'm fixated on a bastard who deserted his family, you couldn't be more wrong."

She inhaled sharply. James spoke as if the wound was fresh. When in fact, it had happened almost three decades ago. "He didn't desert you."

"Of course he did." His raised voice upset Sybbie. "Sorry, munchkin." He stood abruptly, part of his meal uneaten. "I need a shower. After that, I'll probably hit the hay early. Do you and the kid need anything?"

It was barely seven thirty. Obviously, this was his way of telling her he wanted to be alone. That she and Sybbie weren't there to socialize with him. "We're fine," Lila said. "I'll call the pest control people first thing in the morning. I would never have asked you to get involved if I had known this would be the outcome."

"Think of it as a blessing in disguise. If I hadn't started the renovation, you might not have known about the termites until they had done catastrophic damage. Good night, Lila."

When he strode out of the room, she stared at Sybbie, who played with a pile of Cheerios, unfazed by the tension between the adults. "Well, kiddo. I guess it's just you and me."

Lila tidied up the kitchen and cleaned the baby's sticky hands. After that, she took Sybbie into the guest room and sat on the bed with her reading a stack of board books she had ordered from Amazon the morning she realized she was going to become a temporary mom.

Sybbie sat between Lila's legs, her soft, sweet-smelling body tucked in Lila's embrace with simple trust. The future was a scary void. What were they going to do? How could they be a family?

Today during naptime, Lila had begun ticking off a list of calls: her coworkers at the bank, women in her yoga class, friends she had made since she had moved to Silver Glen. Every conversation left her more and more despondent. Apparently, good nannies were very hard to find.

Not only that, but they were expensive. Obviously, if you wanted to hire a young woman with credentials, you couldn't pay teenage babysitter wages. Money aside, it might take several months to locate such a person. Lila didn't have that much time.

She *had* to be at the bank come Monday. Quitting wasn't an option, because then she wouldn't be able to support herself and a child. The only alternative was to cobble together some part-time sitters until she could make a permanent decision about whether or not to keep Sybbie.

Truthfully, she already knew how things were going to play out. This precious, chubby infant shared her DNA. In only a few days, Lila had fallen in love with her. But maybe Sybbie deserved better. Lila wasn't the nurturing type. She worked long hours. And at the very heart of the matter, she was scared—scared to be responsible for someone so tiny and vulnerable.

By the time she had bathed the baby and put her in a fresh diaper and pj's, Sybbie was drooping. Lila laid her down in the crib and turned off the light. "Good night, sweet pea." The baby was already turning onto her tummy and curling into her favorite sleeping position.

Lila closed the door quietly and stood in the middle of her bedroom. She was accustomed to being on her own. Ever since she went off to college, she'd had no one to depend upon but herself. She rarely saw her mother, mostly because her mother made it clear that she didn't want Lila around.

Maybe Lila had made a pest of herself by offering to pay for rehab one too many times. Her mom didn't want to be helped. She didn't think she had a problem, even though at the recent funeral she had been so drunk or medicated or both that she was barely able to stand.

Back when James and Lila had been going out, there was a time when Lila fantasized about becoming a Kavanagh. Not only because James was smart and funny and seriously hot...but because the thought of belonging to the large, tight-knit family made her yearn for something she had never experienced. She didn't know what it was like to always know that someone had your back...that in a crisis you didn't have to face things alone.

Suddenly, a wave of panic swamped her. She had to get out of this house. Grabbing a jacket and the baby monitor, she slipped out the back door. The range on the small electronic device wasn't extensive, but she would go as far as she could and still see the baby.

First, she slipped next door to her own house and surveyed the mess James had made. Her tidy dining room was gone. James had moved the table into the guest quarters that would eventually be Lila's downstairs bedroom.

Everything was coated in a fine film of dust.

How was she going to manage? She didn't know anything about being a parent. Moms were supposed to bake cookies and sew Halloween costumes and host sleepovers. Lila was happiest in a room alone with paper and figures and tasks that she had the skills to do well.

She was exhausted and grieving for her sister and, at the heart of it all, bruised in spirit. Bruised because the one man she had ever really felt deeply about didn't want a woman like her.

The tears, when they came, took her by surprise. But

instead of choking them back, she gave in to the barrage of pain and sorrow and fear. She'd been leaning against a wall. Now she slid to the floor and buried her head on her knees, sobbing until her chest hurt.

Six

James heard the back door open and shut. He watched from the upstairs bedroom window as Lila slipped across the side yard like a shadow. What the heck was she doing?

Don't follow her. His gut was smarter than he was. He needed to keep his distance. Lila wasn't his problem.

Five minutes later he cursed beneath his breath and went after his reluctant houseguest. He found her sitting on the dusty dining room floor, crying as if her heart was broken. His reaction stunned him. All he wanted to do was pick her up and carry her home and make love to her until she understood that everything was going to be okay.

Instead, he kept his distance and cleared his throat. Her head snapped up immediately. "James. What are you doing here? I have the monitor with me. I wouldn't neglect the baby."

Her face was blotched with tears, her nose red and her eyes puffy. "I know that, Lila." She seemed so small and lost and alone. But he knew she was strong and confident and well respected by her peers at the bank. The president had hired her on the day she interviewed for the job. "Maybe it would help to talk about it," he said quietly. "To a neutral third party."

He wasn't neutral about Lila. Probably never would be. The fact that he still cared about her made him a decent human being. Not a guy itching for another round of getting punched in the gut. She wasn't what he needed. He wasn't what she wanted.

Joining her on the floor, he stretched out his legs and sighed. "Let it out, Lila. I make a good confessional, I swear."

In profile, her features were delicately carved. He saw the shuddering sob that signaled the end of her catharsis. Tears were good...for women at least. Sometimes he envied the fairer sex for their ability to express emotion. For him, it was usually chopping wood or hiking seven miles that took the edge off when he felt overwhelmed or sad.

"Talk to me, Lila."

It took a long time, but finally she answered. "I don't think I can keep Sybbie."

Inwardly, he recoiled, but he kept his expression impassive. "Why not?"

"Look at me. You know who I am. I'm not the Martha Stewart type. I'm good at my job, but it requires long hours. That's partly why you and I broke up. I don't want Sybbie to be raised by a nanny. She deserves a traditional home with two parents. You and I both missed out on that. Surely it would be hypocritical of me to keep her when I can't devote my time to raising her myself."

"Can't or won't?"

Lila froze. His sharp question had spewed out uncensored, revealing his visceral reaction to the idea that she would give away her niece. "Thanks for the support," she said.

For a split second he saw anguish in her eyes. He didn't

want to cause her pain, but he also didn't want her to make a decision she would regret later. Carefully, he put a hand on her arm, expecting her to knock it away. Instead, she froze. "I'm not your enemy, Lila. Let me help you." He was trying to reach her through touch. They weren't a couple anymore, but they were neighbors, and surely they could become friends again.

"You're already helping me," she said.

"That's different. You hired me to do a job. Anyone could have done that for you."

"Then what do you mean?"

He squeezed her arm and let go. "I want to talk to you about something, but I'd feel more comfortable if we were closer to Sybbie. Let's go back and I'll pour us a couple glasses of wine."

Lila had hit rock bottom. It was bad enough when she and James broke up. But she'd had her job and her friends to distract her. Tonight, she knew she had disappointed him. Why couldn't he understand that she was proud of her job...that she enjoyed her work?

James surely had gleaned some of his ideas about women from 1960s sitcoms. He wanted a wife who would greet her husband at the door with a baby on one hip and a beer in the other. For him. Of course. His attitude really made no sense, because his own mother had worked her whole life, though admittedly in the family business.

Most of his sisters-in-law had careers. She'd never heard him be judgmental about them. Maybe it was only Lila's life choices he found unacceptable.

In every other way, he seemed to be an enlightened male. But apparently not when it came to the future mother of his yet-to-be-born children.

James was already standing. She pretended not to see his outstretched hand. Instead, she got to her feet and brushed the sawdust from her legs. "Okay," she said. "We'll talk. But I can't see how that changes anything."

She absolutely had to show up for work Monday morning. Taking Sybbie with her was not an option. She was out of answers. Not only did she have zero prospects for a nanny, she had also bombed out when it came to lining up a few temporary babysitters. Of the two problems, the babysitter issue would be easier to solve. If she made another series of phone calls, she could surely find a few dependable people who could tag team during Lila's working hours.

But did she really want to come home from an exhausting ten hours of work day after day and take care of Sybbie? She wasn't a selfish person. Already, she loved the baby. Intellectually, she knew that many families with two working parents made this happen.

The difference was, Lila wasn't married. Once the babysitters went home, she would bear the responsibility for everything else. The thought was not only daunting, it was terrifying.

And that was something James wasn't going to understand. Not unless she told him her secrets. The things that gave her sleepless nights and caused her to wake up in a cold sweat from nightmares.

Stomach churning, she locked her front door and followed him across the yard. With the monitor in her hand, she was reassured that Sybbie was okay. The small, grainy image of the baby kept Lila from imagining the worst-case scenario.

She had assumed James would suggest they sit in his comfy living room to have their drinks. He must have thought that was too cozy, because he took the wine into the kitchen, opened it and poured two glasses. He offered her one and invited her to sit down.

Despite the late hour, there was nothing intimate or

suggestive about the locale. The overhead illumination was bright. The refrigerator hummed quietly.

Finally, she couldn't bear his silence any longer. "You said you wanted to talk." .

He nodded, his long, tanned fingers playing with the stem of his glass. "May I ask you a question?"

"I suppose." Her stomach tightened.

"I honestly thought you didn't like kids, but when I watched you with Sybbie, your face lights up. You are tender and caring and I'm pretty sure you already love her almost as much as if you had given birth to her. Am I wrong?"

"You're not wrong." She'd been trying to decide whether or not to open up all her skeleton-filled closets. James had cut to the chase and simply asked. Flat out. "I do love children," she said. "I always have. And yes... Sybbie stole my heart the first moment I saw her."

"So what's the problem? Tell me, Lila-belle. I want to understand." The goofy nickname was not fair. It made her yearn for a happier time with James.

For her to explain was only going to make it more certain that the two of them were never ever getting back together. Perhaps this was for the best.

"I used to babysit," she said simply. "A lot. From the time I turned thirteen. I took a class offered by the Red Cross at the hospital. Received my certification. I was responsible and dependable and kids gravitated toward me."

"So far, I'm not hearing any negatives."

"I had a very scary experience when I was in the eighth grade. I was babysitting after school for a woman who had a mentally and physically challenged three-year-old. He only knew a few words, but he was extremely sweet and cooperative. His walking was jerky, but he could do it."

"Was this a one-time thing?"

"No. I had a regular job with this lady. She cared for

him all day, and by the time I came to her house after school, she needed a break and a chance to cook dinner for her family. There were two other children and a husband."

"Okay."

James was completely tuned in to her story, his expression intense. She felt like a bug under a microscope. Wine in hand, she jumped to her feet and paced. "One day, the little boy and I were playing with Lincoln logs in the living room. He was old enough not to put little pieces in his mouth."

"But he choked on something."

James's attempt to finish her story made her smile, though there was no humor at all in the memory. "Not exactly. He went into a seizure, fell and bashed his head on the glass coffee table. Blood went everywhere. I screamed. His mother came running and knew immediately what had happened. She told me to call 911, and she held him so he wouldn't hurt himself further."

"You must have been terrified."

"I was. She had never mentioned that he might have a seizure. The whole family made sure I knew it wasn't my fault that he hit his head. But it traumatized me. He could have died. On my watch."

"Is that it?"

She could tell James was waiting to tell her how silly she was…that all kids had accidents. "No. That's not all. The next incident happened two years after that. I was older then. This time I was in charge of three children ranging in age from five to nine. They rode the school bus home together. My job was to give them a snack, make sure they did their homework and sometimes start a portion of the dinner meal before the parents rolled in at five thirty."

"That sounds like a lot for a—what were you? A fifteen-year-old?"

"Yes. But I had been doing it almost four months. The children respected my authority. The parents were thrilled with how smoothly their evenings went after I had been there. I was making good money and socking it away for college."

"Has anybody ever told you your storytelling skills are a downer?" His anticipation of what was coming was accompanied by a rueful grimace.

"You asked for this." It wasn't as if she enjoyed rehashing some of the worst days of her life. "It was getting close to the holidays. The cat got under the Christmas tree and chewed on an electrical cord that was already frayed. The tree skirt caught on fire, but only smoldered at first. Then at some point, the drapes were involved, and after that, the room was engulfed in flames."

"What about smoke alarms?"

"Dead batteries," she said soberly. "It was a perfect storm of bad decisions by the parents…critical things they had overlooked. I was in the back of the house in the den watching TV with the children. When I smelled smoke and tried to get them out of the house, the rear hallway was on fire. Our only escape was through the front door. I had to put wet towels over the kids' heads and hustle them past the flames and out into the yard."

"My God, Lila. That's horrific. Were you hurt?"

"They treated all four of us for mild smoke inhalation. By the time the fire engines arrived, most of the house was engulfed. It wasn't a total loss, but the family had to live in a motel for three months."

She finished her tale and ran out of steam, sitting down abruptly. Even now, years later, retelling the story made her queasy.

James stared at her, his eyes narrowed as if trying to see inside her head. "Is that it?"

Seven

"Isn't that enough?"

James heard the snap in her voice. Maybe he had been trying to get a rise out of her. He wasn't sure why. But if she was still dealing with guilt about things that had happened a decade and a half ago, she needed to let all of it go.

"I'm not sure what any of that has to do with you and Sybbie."

Lila tucked her hair behind her ears. At one time, she'd threatened to cut it. He'd made her swear not to. It wasn't likely that a woman felt bound by a three-year-old promise. Even so, the beautiful blond hair was still long. When she dressed for work at the bank, she wound it up in a complicated chignon that always made him hot.

Lila gave him a look of frustration. "I'm not good in a crisis," she said. "It terrifies me to think of everything that can go wrong when you have little ones to take care of, and that's not even taking into account disease and illness. The accident possibilities alone scare me to death. Especially because I've never cared for a baby. If the experiences I had with other people's children shook me so badly, I don't even want to know how I would react if the kid were mine."

"But you *are* good in a crisis. You just finished telling me how good. I'm not sure I follow your line of reasoning."

"You're a man. Men never worry as much as women do. In your mind, you can handle everything that comes down the pike. But I know better. And I can't live that way. I'd rather stick with my computer programs and spreadsheets. At least I only have myself to worry about."

He was stymied. Though the two of them had argued about everything under the sun when they were a couple, he honestly had no idea how to respond to Lila's irrational fears. Telling her not to worry wasn't a solution.

Because he needed to do something, anything, to break the tension, he stood up and poured himself another glass of wine. "I don't want to see you make a decision you'll regret," he muttered, leaning his butt against the counter. "If you give Sybbie up for adoption, there will be no turning back."

Lila winced as if the A-word was painful. "Children need two parents," she said, her tone dull, as if she were tired of trying to convince herself.

"She's your flesh and blood," he said softly. "You can't let her go, Lila."

"What choice do I have?"

He saw her eyes get shiny and her nose turn red. "There are always choices."

"I'm tired," she said, the words hoarse from her bout of crying. "Tell me what you wanted to talk to me about so I can go to bed."

James gripped his wineglass too tightly; it was a wonder it didn't break. "I want to keep Sybbie for a couple of months. While you're at work."

Lila stared at him, mouth gaping. "Are you insane? No, James. That's ridiculous."

His temper flared, but he kept his words even. "It actually makes perfect sense. And it will give you time to make your decision."

"In case you've forgotten, *you* have a job, too."

"I'm my own boss. I've finished up several big projects recently. If I want to take a break, it's my prerogative. Besides, if I run into any snags, I have my mother and six sisters-in-law I can call."

"What's in it for you? Why would you do this?" she asked bluntly.

He shrugged. "You're a friend, Lila. I'd like to help. You're dealing with grief and an overwhelmingly emotional set of circumstances. I don't want you to do something that can't be undone. I don't want you to live with an aching regret that will haunt you the rest of your life. Yes, I get it. You may in the end give Sybbie up for adoption. If that's what you decide to do, I'll support your decision. But not now. Not so soon. Please. Let me give you some breathing room."

"You're betting on the fact that I'll bond with her and not be able to say goodbye. Isn't that emotional manipulation on your part?"

Her distrust of his motives was insulting, even if she was closer to the mark than she realized. "No games. Not this time. I want you to have the life you need. And I want what's best for Sybbie. I was an ass three years ago, Lila. Let me make it up to you. Let me keep Sybbie so you can go to work and do your job without worrying every minute of every day."

She stared at him for the longest time. For once, her expression was impossible to read. "I think you're crazy, James, but since I'm out of options, I suppose I have to accept your offer."

"You don't *have* to," he said bluntly. "You can pick up the phone, call social services and have them come get Sybbie tomorrow morning. Is that what you want?" He was jabbing the wound, making her face things she didn't want to think about. But what else could he do?

"You don't play fair," she whispered, her eyes shadowed with fatigue and pain.

"I'm not playing at all. I'm dead serious about this." He met her gaze head-on, silently willing her to say yes. He wasn't quite sure why this was so important to him, but it was.

"Okay," Lila said abruptly. "If you're deluded enough to offer, I accept. But I won't be badgered every day. The decision has to be mine. And I'll base my final choice on what is best for my niece. *My* niece, understand?"

James saluted. "Yes, ma'am. Duly noted."

Lila's small smile was wry. "You always did manage to get your own way. It must come from being the baby of the family. You were probably spoiled rotten."

He chuckled. "I don't think you know what it's like to be raised with six older brothers. It's a wonder I survived to adulthood." Lila had visibly relaxed. The mood in the room was no longer critically touch and go. A great relief swept over him. He'd made it past a huge hurdle.

She finished her wine and stood up. "It's late. I need all the sleep I can get." She paused, and he saw muscles in her throat work as she swallowed back tearful emotion. "Thank you, James," she said softly. "I do appreciate your offer."

He straightened and crossed the room before he could change his mind. Without putting his hands on her, he kissed her on the cheek. "You're welcome, Lila. I'm happy to help. Now go to bed and don't dream. Just rest. I'm here if you need me. Everything is going to be okay."

* * *

Despite the drama and the tears—or because of it all—Lila fell into bed and slept like the dead. When she awoke hours later and glanced automatically at the baby monitor, Sybbie was still sleeping. The sun was peeking over the mountain. A new day.

Lila stretched and yawned, realizing with rueful amazement that the knot in her chest was gone—the same tight pressure that had been with her since the moment she got word that her sister had died.

For the first time in days, she felt a fillip of optimism. James, darn his sorry, macho, opinionated hide, was right. She needed breathing room. And he was making that possible. For such a gift, if for no other reason, she owed him a debt of gratitude.

She had little to offer him in return except a blind determination to never let him know how much she still craved his touch. Even that innocent, platonic kiss in his kitchen last night had filled her with an intense yearning for more. She didn't love James. They were too different and too volatile together for that. But she was definitely in lust with him.

In the three years that had elapsed since their painful breakup, she had dated a handful of times and had sex exactly once. Being in bed with another man had convinced her that *no* physical intimacy was better than being with a man who was merely pleasant.

Unfortunately, she knew what it was like to burn...to live and breathe in anticipation of the next moment James would drag her into his bed or hers. Passion—true unadulterated physical hunger—was inconvenient and messy and sometimes scary as hell, but once you had tasted the real thing, other men were pale substitutes.

Shoving those thoughts into a recess deep in the back of her brain, she climbed out of bed and dressed quietly.

With Sybbie still snoozing, there was time for a lifesaving cup of coffee. If she had hoped to run into her host in the kitchen, she was doomed to disappointment. An empty cup in the dishwasher told her that James had been up before her.

She leaned over the sink and tugged the curtain aside for a better view of her house. James stood in the yard, hands on his hips, studying the side of her porch. Suddenly, Lila remembered she had to call the exterminators before the baby woke up. Already in the few days Sybbie had been in her care, Lila had come to see how hard it was to transact any kind of adult business with a baby in tow.

Fortunately, Sybbie remained asleep while Lila dealt with her call. She managed to impress upon the man on the other end of the line the urgency of the situation. He promised to have someone in route within the hour. She texted that information to her host, right about the time Sybbie woke up and made herself known.

Lila went to get her niece and was stopped dead in her tracks by the wave of love that washed over her when she saw Sybbie standing expectantly, her chubby hands clenched on the bed rail. She was already pulling up with confidence, which told Lila the baby would be an early walker.

She picked Sybbie up and snuggled her close. "Good morning, sweetheart." The smell of warm baby was addictive. Sybbie chortled and cooed, pleased to be the center of attention.

After a quick diaper change, Lila decided to leave Sybbie in her pj's for the moment. The morning was cool. She didn't want her charge to get a chill. Besides, the likelihood of smearing breakfast food on a clean outfit was almost a certainty.

The meal in James's kitchen was a lazy affair. So far, Sybbie had eaten everything Lila offered without complaint. Today, she gobbled down bite-size pieces of whole-grain waffle, along with banana circles and milk.

Soon, Lila would have to either go shopping or order some infant items online. The baby was wearing six-to-nine-months clothes, but she was on the big end of the range for her age. The twelve-months sizes were going to be needed sooner than later.

While James was outside making plans with the men who were handling pest control, Lila played on the rug in the living room with the baby. Every time Sybbie pulled up on the coffee table, Lila winced, imagining how badly it would hurt if poor Sybbie fell and hit a sharp corner.

Lila wanted to wrap her in a protective bubble so nothing bad would ever happen to her. Sadly, that wasn't an option. Part of growing up was learning how to deal with hurt, both physical and emotional.

While everything was under control in the short term, Lila couldn't help wondering if James would eventually renege on his offer to keep Sybbie during the daytime. Surely the woman he was dating would think it odd.

On the other hand, Lila knew that the Kavanagh men were products of Maeve Kavanagh's strict guidance. Honor. Responsibility. Trustworthiness. Those qualities had been hammered into seven hardheaded sons. The result was a brotherhood of men who were arrogant and self-assured, but at the same time the kind of men women wanted for the long haul.

But not Lila. Not really. Because she was never going to be the motherly type. Professional women who left the workforce during their childbearing years inevitably lost ground in their chosen fields. And what happened if the marriage didn't work out? The woman would find herself left behind in career advancement and at the same time forced to care for children with an ex-husband who might or might not do his share.

In her gut Lila believed James Kavanagh would never treat a woman so cavalierly. Even so, she knew from watching friends and acquaintances that the *civilized* divorce was the exception rather than the norm. Being a single parent was extremely difficult, which was exactly why Lila was going to think long and hard before she accepted Sybbie on a permanent basis.

James would be disappointed and disapproving if she decided she couldn't handle such a huge responsibility. But Lila had to make that decision for herself. It was the only way.

Eight

James didn't really need to hang around while the pest control techs did their job. But he pretended to have a deep interest in their work to keep from having to go home and share a house with Lila Baxter. She was the only woman who had ever truly dented his heart.

She'd been under his nose for the last three years, but at a safe, neighborly distance. Now they were literally snug and cozy, playing house. It was a dangerous situation for a healthy man in his prime to endure.

He had memories. Lots of them. And a good imagination. It was no trouble at all to visualize Lila naked and warm beneath him while he did wicked things to her beautiful body and drove both of them wild.

Hell. He adjusted himself unobtrusively and tried to concentrate on the supply list he'd been working on. As soon as the termite guys were gone, James was going to head out to the hardware store and pick up a few things he needed to do the work Lila had requested.

When the crew left to take a lunch break, James went

back home to grab his own meal. He found Sybbie in her high chair and Lila microwaving fresh sweet potatoes and green beans.

The baby smiled at him. Lila's greeting was more restrained. "Are you hungry?" she asked, her expression carefully noncommittal. "I found some chicken breasts in your freezer and made chicken salad."

"Sounds great," he muttered. "I'll go wash up."

When he returned, the table was set for two. Lila had located place mats and matching napkins in his jumbled cabinets. Despite her protests to the contrary, clearly she possessed at least a few homemaking genes.

As the adults ate, Sybbie played with a set of aluminum measuring spoons, all five attached to a small silver ring. The baby was loud and verbal, her nonsense syllables the precursor to actual words and sentences. It would be a delight to watch her grow and change. But what did the future hold? What was Lila going to do?

To keep from obsessing about things he couldn't control, he quizzed his nemesis. "You gals doing okay so far?" He wiped his mouth with a napkin and took a long swallow of iced tea.

"Of course," Lila said, her tone mildly insulted. He could swear she stared at his throat. She had nibbled her way down that same sensitive, razor-stubbled flesh on many a day. Three years ago she and James had hiked and ridden bikes and gone dancing, and once the sun went down, they had been all over each other, panting, wanting, making love—sometimes until the sun came up.

Those were heady, wonderful days. But they were over. "I thought you'd want to hear about the termites," he croaked, wincing at his clumsy attempt to carry the conversation.

Lila shrugged. "What about them?"

"The techs are going to drill dozens of holes in the ground around your foundation and in the crawl spaces and who knows where else. Then they'll inject everything they've prepped with hundreds of gallons of pesticide."

"And that's it?"

"They'll come back at regular intervals to check for any living insects, but yeah…that should do it."

"I can't wait to go back home," Lila said.

He frowned. "Am I such a bad host?"

"Of course not. But I know we're in your way."

"Trust me," he said. "You're not."

A heavy silence descended. But Sybbie was adept at covering painful pauses. She reached for James's sleeve. "Da Da," she said clearly.

James froze. Lila was equally dumbstruck.

He cleared his throat. "Must have been a fluke," he said. "She has no clue what she's saying."

The baby held up her arms to be lifted from her seat. "Da Da."

James's face heated. He didn't want Lila to think he was teaching the kid stuff on the sly. But when he looked at Lila he caught an expression of such yearning on her face, he was almost embarrassed to witness it.

Here was a woman who was turning her life upside down to accommodate her dead sister's child, and yet the first words she heard the baby say were *Da Da*. That had to hurt.

He picked up Sybbie and nuzzled her nose with his. Looking over the baby's head, he gave Lila a pointed glance. "What do you want her to call you? Clearly she's getting ready to talk in the next few months. Do you want to be Aunt Lila? Or Auntie? Or plain Lila?"

Lila frowned as she began clearing the table. "I haven't really thought about it."

"How about *Mama*? That's an easy one to say." He was deliberately provoking her, trying to get a reaction.

Lila's glare could have melted snow. "You're pushing your luck, Kavanagh. Don't make me hurt you."

"Promises, promises." His mouth snapped shut, and he felt his face heat. Lila looked stricken. Without meaning to, he had fallen into the teasing banter they used to toss back and forth when they were a couple.

"Sorry," he muttered. "That was out of line."

Lila recovered quickly. "Doesn't bother me," she said breezily. "I got over you ages ago. I'm immune to your deadly Kavanagh charm."

"The hell you say." He was indignant on behalf of all the Kavanagh men. "If I wanted to impress you, I could. You'd be helpless to resist me."

She tossed the wet dishcloth at his head and hit her mark. "Give me the baby and go back to work. Your pompous ego is sucking all the air out of the room."

Laughing, he handed over the squirmy infant and dried his face. "Your loss. You'll miss me when I'm gone."

To Lila's utter chagrin, he was right. The house felt empty without him. She needed to nip this nonsense in the bud ASAP. Her self-esteem was healthy. But she didn't want to test it with another doomed-to-failure attempt at being James Kavanagh's woman.

When the baby went down for her nap, Lila called the bank. Her coworkers had been extremely understanding and accommodating, but with the auditors coming Monday morning, there was a lot of work to be done. She checked in on several items and promised to tie up a few loose ends tonight from home. Once the baby was in bed, she could work from her laptop.

The day passed quickly. There was never time to be

bored with an active, inquisitive infant in the house. Lila was stunned at how quickly her niece was growing and changing. Almost every day, it seemed, Sybbie mastered a new skill. Once she became completely mobile, the challenges in caring for her would escalate.

Despite keeping up with Sybbie, Lila found herself with plenty of time to think. Unfortunately, none of those riveting one-sided conversations brought her any closer to a decision. In her heart, she believed that Sybbie would be better off with a normal, two-parent family. Maybe a situation where the mom chose to stay at home. Or even the dad.

But try as she might, she couldn't visualize a scenario where she voluntarily handed over this precious, blond-headed angel. Even the thought of it made her chest hurt and her eyes burn.

In between moments of soul-searching, she tried to make a dinner plan. Would James be going out? Yes? No? And what should she fix for the baby? Pureed carrots? Smashed peas? In the end, her immediate problems were solved when Mia, Dylan's wife, called to say she was dropping by with some food for tonight's supper. She showed up just after five.

It was great to see a familiar face. Lila hugged Mia and inhaled the wonderful aroma of homemade mac and cheese.

Mia carried the dish to the kitchen. "I just pulled it out of the oven. It will stay hot for at least an hour. I added a broccoli salad and rolls to go with it for you and James. And there's homemade applesauce for the baby."

"Thank you so much. You don't know how much I appreciate this."

Mia took the baby and sat down at the table, bouncing the little girl on her knee. "I think I do. I know what it's like to be a single mom. And you didn't even have nine months to get used to the idea."

Mia had conceived her daughter, Cora, via a sperm donor. It was only later that she met Dylan and the two of them fell in love. Lila nodded. "That's part of what has me so crazy. I'm a planner. This news about my sister came out of the blue."

"It must hurt…even if the two of you weren't close."

Unexpectedly, Lila's throat closed up as tears threatened. She nodded jerkily. "I hadn't seen her in years… not that I didn't try to have contact. I honestly thought she hated me. She used to go on and on about how unfair it was that I was the perfect child and she caught all the flak. It wasn't true, of course. I was far from perfect, but Alicia liked to play the wounded heroine."

"Is there anyone else at all who would take the baby?"

"No one that I know of… My mother can't. I suppose that's why Alicia put my name down as guardian."

"I think she did it because she knew you would do the right thing."

Lila's laugh was hollow. "What *is* the right thing? I wish I knew. I feel like an actress in a bad play who doesn't know her lines."

"From what you've told me about your sister, I'm surprised she even had the foresight to make a will. Isn't that a little odd?"

The same thought had occurred to Lila. "The lawyer said she came to his office on the one day a month he offered pro bono services to the community. Alicia was afraid that if something happened to her, the baby's father would simply walk away. She wanted to protect her daughter."

Mia nodded soberly. "The maternal instinct can be very strong. As it turns out, your sister was smarter than she knew."

"Yes. And I don't want to betray her trust in me, even if she never actually *asked* me to look after Sybbie."

"So what are you going to do?"

Panic threatened, but Lila shoved it back. "Your extremely stubborn and opinionated brother-in-law doesn't want me to make a decision I'll regret later. He's offered to keep Sybbie during the day for the next two months so I can work. He thinks that will give me time to clear my head and ponder all my options."

"I see." Mia's small smile was irritating.

"You don't see *anything*, Mia. There's nothing to see. You remember what things were like three years ago between James and me. We barely had time for a normal dating life. All we ever did was fight and have sex."

"That's more than some couples have." Mia's humor was sly, but Lila refused to squirm.

"This isn't about James and me. We're history. Sybbie is my only concern. She's James's only concern for that matter. So you can wipe that smug grin off your face."

"Yes, ma'am," Mia said meekly, though her eyes still danced.

Lila groaned and covered her cheeks with her hands. "I'm sorry. You brought me this wonderful dinner, and I'm haranguing you."

"Dylan will tell you I had ulterior motives."

"And did you?"

Mia nodded, laughing. "Oh, yes. I couldn't wait to see what was going on over here."

"There's *nothing* going on," Lila cried.

Sybbie's face crumpled, and she started to sob. Mia cuddled her close. "See what you've done? You scared the poor baby."

"Me? You're the one beating a dead horse. I thought you were my friend."

"I *am* your friend, Lila. But I love James, too. I can't

take sides in World War III. I'll be Switzerland and give the child asylum if things get too hot and bothered over here."

"Very funny. There's not a chance in the world that James and I will end up in bed together."

Nine

James walked into the kitchen just in time to hear Lila's impassioned declaration. She really should know better. To a man, especially a horny man, those words were the equivalent of waving a red flag in front of a bull.

Even so, he pretended he hadn't heard her. "Hello, Mia," he said, kissing his beautiful, sweet sister-in-law on the cheek. "Please tell me that's your legendary mac and cheese I smell."

Lila frowned at him. "I assumed you'd have social obligations in the evenings."

"Social obligations?" He played dumb just for the pleasure of seeing her face turn red.

"Dates," Lila said. "With women." The words were clipped and dipped in ice.

He swung a chair around backward, straddled it and joined the two women at the table...three women if you counted Sybbie. "No obligations," he said. "But I'm powerful hungry, ma'am." He smiled at Mia, not Lila, when he said it.

Mia chuckled. "As much as I would like to stay and referee, I have to get back. Dylan's taking me to Asheville tonight for dinner and a concert. You two enjoy the meal and try not to kill each other."

Lila walked her to the front door, feeling an emotion akin to desperation at the thought of being left alone with James. "Here. Give her to me." The feel of Sybbie's sturdy body was a pleasant weight in her arms. "I wish you could stay, Mia."

Mia cocked her head and raised her eyebrows. "Are you actually afraid of him, love? I promise he's domesticated...or at least as much as a Kavanagh male can be."

"It's not him I'm afraid of," Lila confessed baldly. "It's me."

Dylan had followed the two women down the hall, intending to say goodbye to Mia, too. But when he realized the two females thought they were alone, he hung back. Hearing his sister-in-law's question made him frown. But Lila's subsequent answer knocked his socks off. Because it indicated loud and clear that Lila felt the same physical pull he did.

Still, he lingered for a moment in the shadows. What was he going to do with this knowledge? Did he want to end up in bed with Lila? His libido said, *Hell, yes*. Fortunately, though, James was older and wiser now than three years ago. He'd learned a tough lesson. Just because something felt fun and amazing in the short term didn't make it a valid life choice.

That maxim held true for a lot of things. Alcohol in excess, wild monkey sex with his beautiful blonde neighbor, becoming a full-time dad. He had to be smart and cautious in the weeks to come. Lila needed his help, but she didn't want him as a lover. That was a good thing.

He repeated those five words under his breath to remind himself luscious Lila was not up for grabs. She was here in his house as a friend in need. Knowing that she still felt the zing of attraction changed nothing.

Taking a deep breath to still his galloping pulse, he joined the women in the foyer. "Thanks, sis, for the food." He gave her a hug. "You're a wonder. Dylan's a lucky man."

Mia preened adorably. "He is, isn't he? And you're very welcome for the meal. I've gotta run. Talk to you both soon."

When the door closed, James scrubbed his hands across his face. "I'm going to grab a shower. After that I'd be glad to entertain our little princess while you set out dinner. Will that work?"

Lila hesitated visibly.

"What's wrong with that plan?" He sighed, irritated that her first response these days was always negative. "Am I making too many assumptions? Taking charge without asking your opinion? Bossing you around?" Those had been a few of their hot-button issues three years ago.

"Of course not," Lila muttered. "But I don't want you to feel like you have to entertain us. You should go about your business…do whatever you would normally do."

"What if I want to sit on the sofa and watch a movie with a beautiful blonde?"

She blinked, shocked. "Um…"

He chuckled. Turns out, taunting Lila was almost as much fun as having sex with her. "*Ghostbusters* is on one of the classic movie channels." She had made the mistake long ago of telling him she had a secret weakness for old Bill Murray movies.

Lila sputtered but didn't actually answer the movie question. "I have to change Sybbie. Go take your shower. We'll eat in twenty minutes."

James loped up the stairs feeling a burst of energy. He wasn't blind to the pitfalls of his current situation. But did it really hurt anything if he enjoyed Lila's company in the short term?

She was funny and extremely smart. In fact, she had a lot in common with Mia. It was no wonder the two of them had hit it off and remained friends. Maybe he should pick Mia's brain about the current situation.

When he made it back to the kitchen, Lila was crouched on the floor picking up a blob of mac and cheese that Sybbie had bobbled. He poured himself a drink and grabbed two plates out of the dishwasher. "You ready to dig in?"

Lila looked up at him. "I need to give her a bottle and put her down. You start. I'll get mine in a few minutes."

James ate alone frequently. He had no trouble with solitude. But somehow, the anticipation of tonight's meal lost its savor. Despite Lila's admonition, he decided to wait for her. It disturbed him that he was more pumped about this evening's platonic slate of events than he had been when out with his most recent date.

He was a messed-up son of a bitch. His brothers had one by one succumbed to the lure of marriage, because each of them had found women who were perfect for them… matches made in heaven, his mother would say.

James, on the other hand, was mildly obsessed with the one female who was exactly wrong for him. He wanted a family. She didn't. He believed in mixing work with a healthy dose of pleasure. She was a workaholic. He liked to take care of the females in his life. Lila was independent and stubborn and didn't think she needed help.

The only place they had ever really been an even match was in bed.

Don't go there, bro.

His conscience was smarter than he was.

In the midst of his soul-searching, Lila returned with Sybbie. The small child wore blue-and-pink bunny pajamas that made her look like a baby doll. "Let me give her the bottle," he said impulsively.

Lila nodded, her expression hard to read. "Sure." She handed over the drowsy infant and quickly prepared the formula.

James had no qualms about feeding the kid. He had a handful of nieces and nephews, with more on the way. This wasn't his first rodeo.

Lila moved quietly around the kitchen, fixing two plates of Mia's amazing food. Soon, the baby was sound asleep.

"I'll put her in her bed," Lila said.

He stood up carefully. "Let me do it. No point in jostling her more than necessary."

Lila followed him into the office/nursery. The lights were out already. Only a faint glow shone from the hallway.

The two adults stood side by side at the crib. For some reason, James was reluctant to put Sybbie down. There was something about a child's innocence and helplessness that made a man feel important and needed.

For a moment, he flashed back to what must have been no more than a wisp of a memory. He remembered big hands cradling his head and a husky voice singing an Irish lullaby. His father. His irresponsible Peter Pan of a parent. The selfish, thoughtless man who had abandoned a loving wife and seven sons to pursue a fool's errand.

Lila touched his arm. "What's wrong, James?"

He was startled, unaware that his disquiet had been evident to anyone but himself. At another time, in another place, he might have brushed aside her question. Maybe the shadowy room and the glass of wine he'd consumed while waiting for the womenfolk had lowered his defenses.

"I was thinking about my dad," he said gruffly. "I don't remember him, not really. But when I was about to lay Sybbie in her bed I felt a flash of something. I'm not sure.

I was so young back then, it couldn't have been a real memory."

"You don't know that. If the moment was all you had of him, it might have lingered in your subconscious all these years."

"I suppose." He didn't want to think about his father. And he sure as heck didn't want to emulate him. If James were lucky enough to get married and have a family one day, he was going to be the best dad he could be. James's child would never feel the sting of abandonment.

Lila nudged his arm. "I'm hungry. Put her down, James."

He gently laid little Sybbie on her back and watched in amusement as she flipped to her tummy and drew her pudgy legs beneath her. It looked like an uncomfortable way to sleep, but then again, who was he to say?

In the brightly lit kitchen and without the baby as a buffer, the atmosphere became laden with tension…or maybe not so much tension as awkwardness. He and Lila were not bosom buddies. Nor were they lovers. Not anymore. It was difficult to know how to act around her.

So they ate in silence.

Finally, Lila broke the ice. "Are you sure, James? About keeping Lila? You can change your mind. I won't think less of you. Caring for a young child for hours on end is not easy."

"I know that. But if I get in a bind, I have seven women in my life, Mom included, who would be more than happy to give me a hand. It's only eight weeks, nine at the most. The time will fly by."

"And then I'll have to decide what to do."

She was terrified, he realized. Lila thrived on organization and routine. A baby, no matter how amenable, was unpredictable. Was that the problem? Or did Lila really worry about something happening to Sybbie, something terrible?

Lila, by her own admission, knew children and how to care for them. But by that same token, she was aware of the risks.

Toddlers were always bumping into things and falling down. You couldn't seal them up in Bubble Wrap and protect them from the world. Was parenting a scary proposition? Probably so. But people did it all the time. He had to convince Lila that she was Sybbie's best shot at a normal, loving family life.

"Let's watch the movie," he said. "You've had a stressful few days. You should relax."

Lila grimaced. "I have some work I need to do for Monday's audit. My staff has been wonderful while I've been out, but some of this falls to me."

He sighed, wondering whether to push her. "Please, Lila," he said softly. "It's not a long movie. You need to laugh and loosen up. You're wound too tight. Say yes."

He knew she was going to say no. Lila was not the kind of woman who blew off work for a movie. She surprised him by nodding slowly. "You're right. But Sybbie smeared food all over me. I need to change. I'll be right back."

Ten

Lila slipped out of her ruined shirt and jeans and ran a brush through her tangled hair. Her heart beat faster and her respiration was ragged. *It's just a movie*, she told herself firmly. James was being a considerate host. This certainly wasn't going to turn out like the time they watched a French film from the 1960s. On that memorable evening, the two of them had ended up on the carpet, bare-assed, clinging to each other and making love like they were the last two people on a planet about to be destroyed by a giant asteroid.

That was the thing about being with James. Life was never boring.

She found the clean pair of stretchy yoga pants she had packed and topped it with a white button-up shirt. When she looked in the mirror, her eyes were huge, the pupils dilated. What was she doing?

Playing with fire. She knew it, and she didn't even care. She was tired and stressed out, and for once, James's macho tendency to think he always had the answers was not a bad thing.

Making her way to the living room took longer than it should have. She checked on Sybbie multiple times, adjusted and readjusted the baby monitor, washed her face, put on some tinted lip gloss and added a touch of mascara.

At last, she could delay no longer. She found James already sprawled on the sofa, his long legs clad in faded jeans, his bare feet propped on the coffee table. On his top half he wore an ancient dark green Henley shirt. She had seen the man a couple of times in a tuxedo. In formal clothing he looked magnificent. But if she were honest, this was the way she liked him best.

He patted the cushion beside him. "Have a seat."

She didn't want to make a scene about taking a chair instead. No need for him to think she was still affected by him physically. So she perched on the end of the sofa with a safe distance between them. James's lips twitched, but he didn't comment.

The movie was fun, but she had seen it half a dozen times. Her mind wandered inevitably. Her brain kept picking at the Sybbie situation like a sore that would never heal. If she quit her job to care for the baby, she couldn't afford to feed them both. If she kept her job, she would see little of the child, because she often didn't get home until after six.

Sybbie wouldn't turn one for quite a while. Day care was still a good three to four months away, even if Lila got her niece on the waiting list. When a tension headache began tightening a band around her skull, she sighed and closed her eyes. James noticed, of course.

"Turn sideways," he said, the words as raspy as sandpaper.

She did as he asked. Staging a protest would take far too much effort.

James moved behind her and put his hands on her shoulders. "Relax, honey. You're going to make yourself sick if you keep going like this."

When James let his guard down, his Southern accent tended to thicken. Lila loved his voice. It was deep and warm and sexy. When his thumbs dug into the knotted muscles of her upper back, she could have whimpered.

Despite her emotional distress—or maybe because of it—succumbing to the magic of James's touch was beautifully erotic. Even as he massaged the places that were tight—the spots that hurt—she felt herself falling into a cloud of sensual bliss. A funny feeling in the pit of her stomach made itself known. Her thighs tightened, her breasts ached, her nipples beaded beneath her shirt.

"That feels so good," she whispered, the words slurred.

Her eyelids fluttered, but she couldn't lift them. She was so sleepy...

James considered it a personal victory that he had managed to coax the uptight banker into relaxing and falling asleep. He eased her onto her back, her head on his lap. With Lila none the wiser, he was free to winnow his fingers through her hair. It was like golden silk. The long waves fanned across his lap.

With the shape Lila was in, he could seduce her into his bed with no real effort. That wasn't conceit speaking. The kind of sexual attraction that afflicted them both was urgent and inescapable.

But his mother had raised her boys to be gentlemen. And that certainly included not going after what he wanted with a woman who was out for the count. She wasn't intoxicated. But she was vulnerable and emotionally fragile. He wouldn't abuse her trust.

The movie ended and another one began. Should he wake her up? She was sleeping deeply, her lips parted slightly. Her throat was slender and creamy. Her breasts swelled noticeably beneath her shirt. Lila thought her boobs were too big. He thought they were perfect. She was tall, so her hourglass figure suited her.

At last she roused on her own. "I'm sorry," she said, yawning and sitting up. "I didn't mean to do that."

"No worries. It was my pleasure."

Her cheeks turned pink. "I should go to bed." The words were barely a whisper.

He nodded. "I know."

What happened next was inevitable. Later he could never remember who moved first, but it didn't matter. Their lips met and clung in a kiss of lazy, mind-blowing pleasure. He was hard in an instant, but then again, he'd been in that condition most of the time she slept with her head in his lap.

"James…" The word was a startled cry, perhaps joy, more likely consternation.

He moved his mouth over hers, capturing every ragged sigh, each drop of sweet, addictive honey. With one hand he cupped the back of her neck and drew her more deeply into his embrace. He'd forgotten her softness, her eager passion. Her tongue dueled with his. She was no innocent waiting to be tutored. She was a woman—a woman who knew how to turn him inside out.

When he touched her breast, it was entirely involuntary. But as soon as he did it, he recognized his mistake. Lila jerked out of his arms, her expression aghast. She put her hands to her hot cheeks. "Is this what you really meant when you mentioned a movie?"

He kept his temper in check with some effort. "Not at all. But you can't tell me you weren't as involved in that kiss as I was. You liked it, Lila. Admit it."

"I'm sorry," she said, her gaze downcast. "You're right, of course. Good night, James."

Before he could reach for her, she was gone. His curse

was long and fervent. He knew how to calm a skittish horse. But this was different. Were he and Lila merely reliving the past? Or was that flame still alive?

Only time would tell.

Lila cried herself to sleep and awoke with puffy eyes and a red nose. She lay in bed feeling sorry for herself until she heard Sybbie stir. It was impossible to hang on to a gloomy mood with the baby's sunny smile beamed in her direction.

"Good morning, my poppet. Did you have pleasant dreams?" She changed Sybbie's diaper and put her in a sunshine-yellow onesie for the day's activities.

In the kitchen, it was a relief to find James nowhere in sight. She fixed the baby a bottle and sat in the spindle-back rocking chair to give it to her. Then the two of them shared the leftover applesauce on toast while Lila had a cup of coffee.

James's kitchen was warm and welcoming. He'd preserved all of the early twentieth-century charm while adding every modern convenience. It would be a great place to feed children every morning before taking them out to the school bus.

But she didn't want children, did she? The idea of taking on that responsibility for life scared her to death. Imagining Sybbie sick with the flu or something worse made Lila's stomach cramp. Children were fragile creatures. They needed two committed parents to keep an eye on them.

As for Lila, she didn't really need a man in her life. She had a healthy bank balance and a portfolio that was modest, but growing. She would do fine on her own.

None of that explained why she kept fantasizing about playing house with James Kavanagh. Being here derailed her common sense.

About the time she came to that conclusion, James showed up and headed for the sink to wash his hands. He was covered in dirt to his elbows.

"What have you been up to?" she exclaimed. It was barely eight thirty.

"I'm planting a couple of dogwoods near the street. I wanted to get it done before the pest control guys get here."

"About that," she said, wincing. "I just got a text from the company dispatcher. They have several guys out sick. They had to cancel my job today."

"I'm sorry, Lila."

She shrugged. "At least you can have a day to deal with your own to-do list. If they come tomorrow, do you think you can finish up my small renovation quickly? Will I be able to go home in a couple of days?"

James dried his hands and leaned against the sink, arms crossed over his chest. "Tomorrow is Saturday, Lila. The termite guys don't work on the weekends. Which means they'll hopefully be here Monday to pump all the liquid into the holes they drilled yesterday. Then I think the house has to sit for twenty-four hours before I can do any more woodwork. By then, I'll be keeping Sybbie during the day. I'll only be able to work on your house in the evenings. If we're lucky, I can finish everything up by the end of next week."

It was quite a speech. And it effectively obliterated her hopes of getting out from under James's roof anytime soon. "Well, that's just peachy," she muttered.

"I'm sorry."

"It's not your fault."

He grinned. "I know. But you wish it *were*, so you could have somebody to yell at."

Even she could see the humor in the situation. "That *would* make me feel better." She smiled reluctantly. This wasn't the end of the world. Surely she and James could coexist for a few more days.

"We're not going to have sex with each other," she said firmly.

His eyebrows went to his hairline. "Did I miss something?"

"Don't play coy with me, James Kavanagh. You know what I'm talking about. We have some sort of weird magnetic attraction between us, but I have too much on my plate right now to be reading a page from the past with you."

"I see."

"You agree with me…don't you? We were terrible together. No reason to make ourselves miserable again."

"If you say so."

His tone was deliberately patronizing and patently insincere. She wanted so badly to smack him that her hand actually trembled. He clearly got some kind of weird, twisted pleasure out of making her lose her temper. But that kind of game played both ways. "If you can't work on my house until after Monday, then Sybbie and I should go home for the weekend."

James's face turned red. "Don't be ridiculous. I've trashed your downstairs. There's dust and pieces of Sheetrock everywhere."

"We'll make do."

James straightened to his full six foot three inches. His brown eyes glowed with heat. "I forbid it," he growled, his voice hoarse. "For a smart woman, you're being completely unreasonable."

Sybbie was in her high chair. Which left Lila free to stalk to where James stood and go toe-to-toe with him. Unfortunately, that put her nose at his top button. She tipped back her head. "You *forbid* it?" she said, her tone incredulous. This was three years ago all over again. Had they learned nothing in the interim? "I was right all along. You really are a bossy know-it-all."

James picked her up as if she weighed no more than Sybbie and set her on the counter. Then he moved between her legs and put his arms on either side of her. "I'm trying my damnedest to take care of you," he said, his exasperation unmasked. "Do you remember all those first responders who got sick after 9/11? Breathing in demolition particles can be toxic, especially for a baby. You're staying right here."

"You can't tell me what to do." Lila clung to her defiance. But it wasn't easy. James's eyes were even more beautiful up close. And she could see a tiny nick where he had cut his chin shaving. His body was big and warm and totally beautiful...in a masculine, macho kind of way.

He shuddered as if a ghost had walked over his grave. "You drive me nuts, Lila."

"The feeling is mutual." She inhaled the scent of his shower soap. "I really want to hate you, James."

"Maybe you should try harder." He leaned his forehead against hers. "I propose a truce."

"How would that work exactly?" If Sybbie weren't in the room, Lila was pretty sure she'd be sliding her hands underneath James's shirt right about now.

"We'll be nice to each other."

"Being nice to each other last night was not a good idea at all."

James cupped his hands on both sides of her neck and stroked her cheeks with his thumbs. His gaze locked on to hers, making it impossible to look away. "It was pretty damned awesome, Lila. But you're right. This is a critical time in your life. I don't want to be the guy who messes with your head when you have big decisions to make. I'm not going to let you do it alone, though. I know you think you can deal with everything on your own, and maybe you can. The thing is, you don't need to. Because I'm here."

For long seconds they stared at each other. Sybbie babbled in the background. Her innocent noises barely registered. Lila was breathless, yearning. If she couldn't have James Kavanagh forever, at least she could enjoy the fruits of his generous nature. "I accept," she said softly. "Thank you, James."

He kissed her nose. "It's the least I can do. Besides, little Sybbie has stolen my heart, too."

Eleven

Retreat was not his usual style. James was more of a *damn the torpedoes, full speed ahead* kind of guy. But this situation required finesse. So despite every instinct to the contrary, he stepped away from Lila.

She hopped down from the counter and busied herself tidying the kitchen. James wasn't fooled. Her hands were shaking and her face was flushed. They were playing a dangerous game. But it wasn't a game. Not really. Little Sybbie and her uncertain future were at the center of James and Lila's impromptu reunion.

The two females were living with him for only one reason, and that reason wasn't so James and Lila could fall back into a physical relationship. As much as he wanted to push for more, he couldn't. He'd promised Lila his support. Bedding her, enjoyable as that would be, was not the answer.

Being a sensible, mature adult sucked.

What was the trio of them going to do for the next three days? There were a few small things he could tackle at

Lila's house, but that wouldn't take more than an hour and a half.

Lila interrupted his pondering. "You have a life, James. Even if the baby and I have upended your routine. Go. Do whatever it is you would normally do on a weekend. I'll spend some quality time bonding with my niece."

She was kicking him out of his own damned house. "What if I don't want to go?" he asked. The question came out more sharply than he intended.

Lila paled. "Please do. I need time to think, and I can't do it with you around."

He didn't know whether to be pissed or jubilant. Lila might not want him underfoot, but she wasn't indifferent. "Fine." He ran his hands through his hair, trying to focus. All he wanted to do was kiss Lila again. He wanted that a lot. Instead, he cleared his throat. "I have some family obligations, anyway. Call my cell if you need me. Otherwise, I'll see you Sunday night to make plans for the week."

Lila blinked. "Sure."

"Isn't that what you wanted?" He scowled at her, unwilling to be jerked around by his own unfortunate, ill-timed hunger.

"Of course," she said, the words oddly flat.

"You can't have it both ways, Lila. I'm not your platonic friend. I'm an ex-lover and a current neighbor trying to help you with a tough situation. I'm a healthy, heterosexual man. You're a beautiful, desirable woman. If we keep this up, we're going to end up in bed. So I'm outta here."

She nodded, tears glittering in her eyes. "I understand. Sybbie and I will be fine on our own."

When James was upset, he went to the woods, sometimes with one of his brothers. Today, though, he'd be lousy company for anyone. So he headed out alone. Ever since he was seven or eight years old, he'd hiked these trails again and again. The mountain was no stranger to him. She held no fears. James pushed himself hard, sweating and panting as he climbed uphill and down at breakneck speeds.

It was a beautiful autumn day—the air crisp, the sunshine warm, the leaves on the trees just starting to change color. But he barely saw any of it. He felt like he was racing his demons, and the demons were winning.

His lungs burned, his muscles ached and still he wanted Lila. She was like an infection in his blood. Malaria, maybe. For three years he had been symptom-free. Now, suddenly, he had a full-blown case of the fever.

When he tripped over a branch and nearly took a header down a steep embankment, he came to his senses. It would help no one if he ended up in a cast. The eight or nine weeks of child care he had promised Lila were going to be challenging enough without adding a broken limb to the mix.

He found a spot under a tree and sat down, legs sprawled, chest heaving. This forest was his temple. The place where he came to commune with the Almighty and find forgiveness and peace. It wasn't easy being the youngest of seven boys. For the first part of his life, he'd brawled his way though most situations, trying to prove he was as strong and as fast and as capable as his siblings.

Then came the day when he outgrew and outweighed the rest of them. He was built like a lumberjack. He didn't understand his own strength...until the afternoon he and Gavin had gone at it about some long-forgotten disagreement. The two of them had used fists and kicks and everything else until they had both been bloody and worn.

James's life changed forever when he landed a punch and Gavin went down hard, striking his head on a rock. For three days, James's brother lay unconscious in a hospital room. When Gavin finally woke up—thank God with no lasting damage—James decided he was done with fighting. He learned to channel his temper in other directions…to control it and not be controlled *by* it.

The truth was, though, he still enjoyed a good fight, even if those conflicts were now verbal.

At first, his brothers hadn't understood the change in him. He'd simply refused to be drawn into a physical skirmish, no matter the provocation. Over the years, his family had come to understand his reticence to be involved in violence where he might hurt someone. They'd nicknamed him the "gentle giant." Everyone thought he didn't know, and he didn't let on.

It was actually sweet and kind of funny, because he didn't *feel* gentle at all. His temper had a short fuse, especially with someone like Lila, who pushed his buttons time and again. Back when they'd been dating, he'd either wanted to spank her or strangle her or take her hard and fast up against a wall until neither of them could walk.

He'd mellowed as he got older. It took more to set him off. Most people would describe him as a laid-back kind of guy. So why was he letting Lila get to him so easily?

The answer was alarming. He still wanted and needed her. Quite desperately, as a matter of fact.

That admission shook him. He didn't like being vulnerable, especially not with a woman. He forged his own path in life, paved his own road. He liked calling the shots. His way was almost always the best way.

Unfortunately, Lila wasn't likely to admit that, even if it were true. Three years ago she'd called him bossy and arrogant. It was a good bet he hadn't changed in that regard.

Gradually, the sough of wind in the treetops and the twitter of birdsong calmed his galloping pulse. He concentrated on breathing evenly, feeling the clean air inflate his lungs…exhaling slowly, allowing his aggravation with Lila to melt away.

He'd been telling the truth when he said Sybbie had stolen his heart. All babies were cute. But this one in particular did something to him. She was part of Lila, flesh of her flesh, bone of her own. Maybe that was it. Maybe in Sybbie, James saw the possibilities for Lila…with Lila.

If he were brutally honest, he hated the thought of Lila giving up her niece. Sybbie needed her. Didn't that count for something? The knowledge that Lila might choose to give the child up for adoption was a physical pain in his chest.

Why did he care so much? What was it to him?

As he sat in silence, the disturbing answer floated to the surface of his conscious thoughts. If Lila gave away baby Sybbie, who shared her DNA, that abandonment would be the same thing as James's father walking away and never coming back.

His fists clenched on his thighs. Damn it.

Emotion flattened him out of nowhere, choking him, making his eyes burn. Somewhere in the midst of these far-flung, rugged rocks and woods and hills and ravines lay the pieces of a broken man, a man who'd never lived to see his infant son grow to manhood.

That knowledge had eaten away at James for years. Pain threatened to cripple him. He wanted to rail and shout and pummel something, but he sat rigid, completely still, subduing the beast that threatened to tear him limb from limb. He would not be mastered by his own anger and despair.

He wouldn't give his ne'er-do-well parent that satisfaction, even posthumously.

At last, he found a measure of control. Nothing had changed. James was still the same man. He had a family to love and who loved him. His work gave him great pleasure and personal satisfaction. Lots of people never knew their fathers. It was regrettable but not uncommon.

With a groaning sigh, he got to his feet and stretched.

If he had to stay away from his own home for a few days, he might as well make his mother happy. She scolded them when she thought her "babies" didn't come around often enough.

Fortunately, he had fallen into the habit of keeping a change of clothes up at the hotel. And it was handy that his brother's office had an en suite bathroom with a shower. Liam, the oldest of the Kavanagh brood, ran the hotel alongside their mother, Maeve, who was in her early sixties and showing no signs of slowing down. Liam had been forced to grow up fast when their father disappeared. Even now, he was ultraresponsible and a bit on the sober side.

Dear Zoe, the delightful free spirit whom the family loved dearly, had burst into Liam's life some time ago and showed him there was more to life than work. After that, it was as if Cupid went to work on the Kavanaghs one by one. Now all of Maeve's boys were happily married. Except for James.

He was still young. Maeve didn't nag overtly. But he knew he was on her radar.

He changed into a clean button-down shirt and a pair of khakis. Combing his damp hair, he stared in the mirror. But it wasn't his own reflection he saw. It was blond hair and blue eyes and a face that was beginning to haunt his dreams. His relationship with Lila had ended three years ago. Definitively. He hadn't been pining away for her. Not at all.

Or had he been lying to himself all along?

Twelve

Lila fell more in love with her niece with every passing day. Sybbie was sunny-natured and already had a sense of humor. She liked to play peekaboo and patty-cake and any other game Lila could dredge up from memory.

Because the weather was so nice, Lila put the baby in her car seat, and the two of them went shopping for a jogging stroller. She flinched at the cost, but she needed exercise, and this was a way to kill two birds with one stone.

Though the weekend hours went by quickly, she was keenly aware of James's continued absence. True to his word, he had disappeared. The remainder of Friday, all day Saturday and so far on Sunday, as well. But Lila knew he had at least *slept* at home. She heard him prowling around in the wee hours of the night, and there was always a pot of coffee going when she got up with Sybbie in the mornings.

Now it was late afternoon and Lila's paid time off was drawing to a close. It would be strange to go to work tomorrow. In the last three weeks, her world had been turned upside down.

Losing her sister. Arranging a funeral. Getting to know Sybbie. Packing up the child's things and loading them into the car for the move to Silver Glen. Not to mention reconnecting with James. It was no wonder Lila was rattled and off her game.

She had run two miles today, so now she slowed her pace, cooling off before returning to the house. Sybbie had napped earlier and was happy to be entertained by the passing scenery. Even when a yappy little dog escaped its owner and charged up to the stroller, Sybbie chortled and smiled, rather than being afraid. She was a resilient child. Did she know her mother was never coming back? Or her father?

Lila's heart ached for her niece, who would never remember her parents. Lila could identify. Her dad was little more than a faded image in an old photograph. It would have been nice to have a father while growing up. For Lila, Alicia's dad had been an indifferent stepparent at best. He barely acknowledged his own flesh-and-blood daughter, much less his wife's "brat from another marriage," as he liked to say.

"Oh, Sybbie," Lila said as they walked up the path to James's front door. "What is Auntie Lila going to do? Am I enough for you? Should I let some happy couple have you and love you as much as I do?"

Sybbie babbled, but didn't offer any concrete suggestions.

Lila had her key out, prepared to let herself into the house, when the door swung backward suddenly and James stood there framed in the opening. "It's about time," he said. "I thought you'd been kidnapped by aliens. Your car is still in the driveway."

Seeing him was a punch to the heart, but she kept her cool. "No aliens today," she said, smiling. "I told them I was far too busy for space travel right now. But we did see

Mrs. Carvani's three-legged cat. The poor thing is skin and bones. I think she forgets to feed him."

James unfastened the straps and lifted Sybbie out of the stroller. "She also forgets to button her robe and to wear undies. Half the neighborhood kids have been scarred for life."

Lila shook her head and grinned, happy to see that James was in a lighthearted mood. She was too nervous about tomorrow to deal with any other drama right now.

Once they were inside, he eyed her from head to toe, his gaze lingering on the sweat-dampened curves of her breasts. She was wearing a sturdy Lycra top, but even such a garment had trouble corralling her assets. "Quit staring," she muttered.

James gave her a mocking smile. "My bad." He flicked the end of her ponytail. "You ready for supper?"

"I'm starving," she said. "But I've pretty much decimated the contents of your fridge. I suppose one of us has to go shopping."

James blanched. "I hate the grocery store. What if I take the two of you to the Silver Dollar Saloon for burgers and fries? Dylan has started stocking Kobe beef and the flavor is astounding."

He remembered her tastes well. "I do love beef," she said. "But what about Sybbie?"

"Can't you take baby food for her? I know you like to give her fresh stuff, but this once won't hurt."

"That will work. Do you mind playing with her while I take a quick shower?"

He waved her away. "Go. Get beautified. Miss Precious and I will be in the living room playing with blocks."

Lila raced through her shower, blow-dried her hair and took a shot at some mascara and eyeliner. When she was dressed in skinny jeans and an oversize fisherman's sweater, she grabbed her wallet and phone and took one last glance in the full-length mirror on the back of the bedroom door.

James had dressed casually, so she followed suit. She wanted to look nice. Dylan's watering hole was a favorite of visitors and locals alike. Though it was Sunday night, there would still be a respectable crowd of patrons.

She bounded down the stairs, pausing to admire the high sheen on the newel post. James had poured a lot of man-hours into restoring this house. It was warm and welcoming and full of personality.

At the entrance to the living room, she stopped short, her feet unable to move a single step forward. James was on his back in the floor with the baby sitting on top of him. They were playing ridey horsey.

Seeing Sybbie's face, hearing her childish laugh, the was reward for all the complications the past days and weeks had brought. The baby was healthy and well-adjusted. Hopefully, her life would not be permanently marked by the tragedy that had brought her into Lila's life.

But it was the man on the floor who elicited the strongest emotions at the moment. James's masculine features had softened as he played with his charge. In his expression, Lila saw tenderness, enjoyment and contentment.

The picture shouldn't have made sense. The big macho guy and the tiny toddler he barely knew. Yet somehow, James and Sybbie looked perfect together. Lila's heart swelled in her chest. Without warning, the incomprehensible truth stared her in the face. She loved James Kavanagh. Or she was falling in love with him. Or maybe she had always loved him, but she was only now mature enough to see their relationship for what it was.

The news wasn't happy. James certainly wasn't on the same page. He might feel lust when he looked at her, but that was a poor foundation for forever. If they couldn't be in the same room without arguing, how would they ever be anything more than semihostile neighbors?

She wasn't about to be available for booty calls. And now there was Sybbie to consider. A complication she could not have foreseen, but one she would never wish away.

For several long moments she allowed herself the pleasure of watching the man and the child. What would it be like if they were all a family? The dream was so real she pressed a hand to her chest where her heart ached.

She must have made some noise, because James lifted his head and craned his neck. "That was fast," he said. "And you look beautiful. What a woman."

The compliment was suspect in its effusiveness, so she didn't put much stock in it. "I'm ready whenever you are. We'll take my car because of the car seat, but you're welcome to drive."

James hopped to his feet, nuzzling Sybbie's neck and making her laugh. "Thanks."

Fortunately, it was a quick trip, because Lila couldn't think of a thing to talk about other than platitudes concerning the weather. That topic was exhausted in less than thirty seconds. Afterward, she stared out the window and tried not to notice how good James smelled.

The saloon was noisy and filled with music. Which meant Lila didn't have to worry about the baby bothering other diners. After they ordered, Dylan showed up and plopped down in an empty chair. "How are you two lovebirds doing?" he asked with a smug grin on his face.

Lila expected James to respond with some sarcastic rejoinder, but instead, his face darkened. "Stay out of it, Dylan. Mind your own damn business."

Dylan clearly enjoyed getting his baby brother's goat. The older Kavanagh put his hands lightly over Sybbie's ears. "Children present," he said. "Watch your language, bro."

For some reason, James wasn't in a mood to be teased. Lila intervened. "Where's your beautiful wife, Dylan?"

He leaned his chair back on two legs and sighed. "She's watching over home and hearth. I'm a lucky bastard. Which is why I'll be headed that way in a few minutes. Anything special you-all want before I go? A quiet room upstairs, perhaps?"

Lila jumped in so James wouldn't say something he'd regret. "You know James and I aren't dating anymore, Dylan. Quit aggravating your brother. James is helping me with Sybbie. I'm sure Mia told you the tale."

"She did." Dylan nodded. "But she didn't mention how cozy the three of you are getting."

"Bite me," James said in a voice that told Lila he was grumpy and not in a mood to take his sibling's joking remarks lightly.

She touched Dylan's arm. "I *would* love one of your famous vanilla shakes. Do you have time to make it for me? With the little rainbow sprinkles and whipped cream on top?"

Dylan's smile was rueful. "Of course. You deserve something for putting up with my ornery brother."

"He's not ornery," Lila said, indignant. "You're baiting him on purpose."

James glowered even more. "I don't need a woman fighting my battles."

"Well, excuse me," Lila said sarcastically. "I'm sure I can find something more useful to do than have dinner with a cantankerous, bullheaded Kavanagh."

James touched her wrist. "I'm sorry. I'll behave."

Dylan snorted. "Doubtful."

"Oh, for heaven's sake," she said, exasperated. "Go

away, Dylan. You're not helping matters. Unless you do what I say, I'll call Mia."

Her ultimatum worked. Dylan blanched. "Don't be hasty. I'm going. And dinner's on me."

"Is that supposed to make up for you being an asshole?" James's temper was still volatile.

Dylan bristled. "I don't know what's gotten into you, baby brother, but if you weren't kin to me, I'd kick you out of my bar."

James rose to his feet, his stance militant. "You could try."

Lila inserted herself between the two men, facing James. "Stand down, cowboy." She moved closer to him, her voice barely a whisper. "What in the heck is wrong with you? When I came home earlier, you were all smiles."

He swallowed, his shoulders relaxing a millimeter. "Does the term 'sexual frustration' mean anything to you? Our situation, yours and mine, is complicated. I don't want anyone, much less my brother, taking cheap shots."

Lila put her hand, palm flat, on his chest. "Dylan always has your back. You know that. And I don't mind a little teasing. You have to admit it's funny. You're probably the last person on earth anyone would see as my savior."

"Hardly a savior," he muttered. "Maybe a knight in shining armor."

Her lips twitched. "Apologize to your brother. Please. I can't cause a rift in the Kavanagh family. I'm pretty sure that's an unforgiveable offense."

"Fine." James glanced over her head at Dylan, who stood like a statue, his eyes round. "Sorry, Dylan. It's been a long week. I'm a little on edge."

Dylan held up both hands. "No worries, man. Mia made me nuts, too, when we first met. I understand."

Suddenly, every bit of tension drained out of James's

body. Inexplicably, he laughed, a genuine guffaw. "Women. Can't live with them, can't live without them."

Lila was nearly squished when the two brothers grabbed each other in a back-pounding bear hug.

"They're insane," she whispered to no one in particular. "That's the only way I can explain it."

Thirteen

James knew Lila was confused. Hell, he'd confused himself. On paper, it had seemed like a good idea to get out of the house. But when Dylan showed up and began making uncomfortable jokes, James suddenly realized that he liked having Lila and Sybbie to himself.

Now he had to make amends for his erratic behavior. He couldn't blame his bad humor on the fact that he was horny as hell, even if it *was* true. "I think I need to eat," he said meekly. "My blood sugar must have bottomed out."

Dylan nodded soberly. "Yep. I'll bet you're right. It could have happened to anyone."

James locked gazes with his brother, and they both burst into laughter…again. They laughed so hard their faces turned red and their eyes were wet.

Lila shook her head and leaned down to kiss Sybbie on her cheek. "They're wild, untamed creatures, my love. I don't expect you to understand anytime soon. I've known them both for longer than you, and I still haven't a clue."

James finally caught his breath. "Okay. I'm good. Thanks, Dylan. I'll take a shake, too."

Lila, hands on hips, glared at both of them. "That's it? You're all mellow now? Good grief. And people call women moody…" She sat back down, a look of bewilderment and disgust on her face.

James squeezed her shoulder. "I'll help Dylan with the shakes. You and Sybbie hang out and enjoy the music."

Dylan led the way to the back, where they scooped out ice cream and dumped it into frosty glasses. As they worked side by side, Dylan quizzed him. "So what's really going on? I thought you and Lila couldn't be in the same room with each other."

"It's complicated."

"I'm a pretty smart guy. Try me."

James shrugged. "She needed my help."

"I got that part. But what about the fact that you want to jump her bones? Does she know you're panting after her?"

"She knows," James replied glumly, licking chocolate ice cream off his thumb. "We've both agreed that little Sybbie's needs have to come first right now."

"Very admirable. You want me to stitch that on a sampler for you?"

James glared. "You're supposed to be offering me sage advice."

"Since when?" Dylan hooted. "You wouldn't let any of us help you when you were three years old. Why start now?"

"Hand me the sprinkles and quit being a tool. I'm stuck, man. Three years ago when Lila and I ended things, I knew it was for the best. Now… I'm not so sure."

"Don't let her lead you around by the balls."

"It's not like that."

"Then what is it?"

James swallowed hard. "I think I might want more than sex from her."

"Like a ready-made baby and a white picket fence?"

"Yeah. Is that weird?"

"Maybe. You're young. You're free. Why muck up the perfect bachelor life with chains?"

"That's changing your tune. Ever since you met Mia and married her, you've been disgustingly happy and smug."

"True. But Mia's one of a kind."

"I'd put my Lila up against her any day," James snapped.

Dylan chuckled. He took the can of whipped cream and squirted a fancy mountain on top of Lila's shake. "I was testing you, man. You passed. Clearly, this woman means something to you…and the kid, too. If it's what you want, go for it."

James nodded, but he hadn't told Dylan the whole story. The problems James and Lila had battled three years ago were still there…just beneath the surface. What was he going to do about that?

Back at the table, Lila was feeding Sybbie a jar of strained peaches. James wrinkled his nose. "Looks delicious."

"Shh," Lila said. "She's smart. I don't want her to learn sarcasm so soon."

He chuckled. "Kids pick up all sorts of stuff they shouldn't. But most of us turn out all right in the end."

"If you say so."

"Was that a snide comment about my character?"

She lifted an innocent eyebrow. "If the shoe fits."

A server appeared right about then, bearing the burgers and fries and saving James the trouble of finding a suitably crushing retort. He had always loved sparring with Lila.

A few of Lila's friends stopped by the table to say hello and offer their sympathies. Clearly, they were interested in meeting Sybbie, too. The grapevine was alive and well in Silver Glen. It would be hard to keep a secret even if you tried.

After that, the meal was consumed mostly in silence, save for Sybbie's vocalizing. But the baby was winding down. By the time the two adults finished off their calorie-laden comfort food, Sybbie's eyelids were heavy.

"We'd better get her home," Lila said. "I don't want to disrupt her schedule. She's been such a good sleeper the past week it would be a shame to mess that up."

James nodded. "It's chilly outside. I'll bring the car to the door." With no bill to pay, they didn't have to wait around. Dylan had said his goodbyes and had headed home to his family.

Outside, the skies were dark. No moon. Only the twinkle of a million stars. James started the engine and turned on the heater. It was that time of year when the days were balmy, but the nights could be frosty. When he pulled to the front and helped put the baby in the car, he was struck by the normalcy of it all. He and Lila, together again, and a baby.

But the picture was a sham. He and Lila hadn't made it as a couple, and little Sybbie might not even be staying in Silver Glen. His enjoyment in the simple evening faded, especially since Lila hadn't said a single word since they'd left the Silver Dollar.

Back at the house, he didn't offer to help with Sybbie's nighttime routine. He needed time to think. Not only that, he was suddenly uncomfortable with the faux domesticity. Just because the rest of his siblings were happily married didn't mean James was ready to follow in their footsteps.

If he made a mistake, the relationship could end in divorce. The Irish Kavanaghs had been Catholic for centuries back. His mother would be heartbroken if one of her sons broke the sacred covenant of marriage.

And there were other factors to consider. In all honesty,

Sybbie really would be better off with an adoptive family if James and Lila tried to make things work and failed. Children needed stability.

When Lila finally joined him in the den forty-five minutes later, her mood was hard to decipher. She looked tired, her normal positive energy dimmed. There was no question of sharing the sofa tonight. They each chose chairs across from one another.

"Is she asleep?" he asked.

Lila nodded. "Before I finished the last storybook."

"Good."

The awkwardness of the conversation registered a ten plus. So many things they weren't saying. James stifled his frustration. "Tell me your schedule for tomorrow, so we're both on the same page. And please don't ask me again if I'm sure. I wouldn't have offered to help with Sybbie if I didn't want to."

Lila grimaced. "Okay. I'll need to leave for work around eight o'clock. I'm usually home after six, but with the auditors there, I won't know for sure."

"That's not a problem."

"While she slept this afternoon, I made a spreadsheet of her schedule. Stuff like meals and snacks and naptime and how often she needs her diaper changed. Plus, there's a PDF with additional information about clothing and medicine and emergency numbers."

James couldn't help himself. He crossed the room and sat down on the ottoman in front of her chair. "I always loved that about you," he said. "You could organize a natural disaster without breaking a sweat."

She seemed nervous having him so close. "Are you making fun of me, James?"

"Never. I think you're amazing." He took her hands in his. The feminine ones were cold and trembling. "I swear to you, Lila, I'll guard Sybbie with my life. You have nothing to worry about. Nothing at all. I know you think I'm arrogant, but this is different. If I find myself in over my head, I'm not too proud to ask for help. I have a big family, any one of whom is usually ready to interfere on a moment's notice."

She smiled faintly. "Don't you mean *ready to help*?"

He rolled his eyes. "With Kavanaghs, it's the same thing."

"Then thank you. That's very comforting. Will you text me every so often? Just so I'll know what's going on? I may not be able to answer, but it would make me feel better about abandoning her."

"You're *not* abandoning her," he said firmly. "You're working to support her and sharing your sweet bundle of joy with a friend."

Lila's eyes glittered with tears. "Why are you doing this?" she asked huskily.

His grip tightened on her slender fingers, trying to warm them. "For Sybbie. For you. Maybe even for me. A guy needs to do a good deed now and then to even up the balance sheet. Stars in my crown and all that."

Lila stared into his eyes as if seeking answers to questions they were both afraid to ask. "You're a very special man, James Kavanagh."

He rubbed the backs of her hands with his thumbs. "That's not what you thought three years ago." Even now, the memory of her walking out on him stung. Their breakup had been mutual in theory. But he had the distinct impression she'd judged him and found him wanting.

Lila's fingers clung to his. "Three years ago we were riding high on hormones or pheromones or some full-moon-induced lunacy. We've both grown and changed."

"Enough to try again?" The words slipped out uncensored. Honest to God, he hadn't known he was going to say them.

Lila paled. She bit her lip so hard he was sure it was going to bleed. "James…" She trailed off.

"What?"

"I can't. Not right now. Until I make a decision about Sybbie, what *I* want doesn't matter."

"I see." Disappointment churned in his gut.

"Do you really?" she asked earnestly. "Because I don't want to hurt you. Or either of us for that matter. You matter a great deal to me, James. I want you to know that."

He kept his smile with an effort. "Fair enough. You always were the levelheaded one of the two of us."

Fourteen

Lila knew her defenses were down. The thought of going to work tomorrow was daunting. She had grieved for her sister far more than she realized. And it wasn't a clean grief. She was angry with Alicia for making such a mess of her life. For dumping an innocent child on Lila with no warning.

Then, of course, those thoughts brought guilt. Lila adored Sybbie. Unconditionally. But the choices she had to make in the days ahead weighed on her like an enormous elephant on her back.

She was scared and tired and she needed comfort. "Will you think badly of me if I ask you to hold me?" she whispered.

James's gaze held so much empathy and concern, she felt stripped raw. "Of course not."

Without asking, he scooped her up and carried her to the sofa. They sat together, side by side, with his arms around her. She buried her face in the warm cotton of his shirt. It smelled like him. Familiar and wonderful.

Time passed. It could have been seconds. Minutes. Hours. She drew courage and strength from James's silent, steady presence. She'd felt dangerously close to the edge, but gradually, she calmed. She could do this. Whatever the outcome, she could handle it.

At last, she pulled away. Looking up at him, she searched for any clue as to what he was thinking. But his whiskey-brown eyes held no answers. "Thank you," she said quietly.

He hugged her and released her almost immediately, but not before kissing the top of her head. "Go to bed, honey. Get some sleep. Everything will look better in the morning."

As it happened, for once James was dead wrong. Everything looked worse in the morning. Lila was up four times during the night with a fretful Sybbie. The child was probably teething, though her timing couldn't have been worse. With the auditors coming today, Lila needed to be on top of her game. Instead, she was sleep-deprived, scattered and stressed to the point of snapping.

When Sybbie finally dozed off again at five thirty, Lila decided there was no point in going back to bed. She showered and fixed her hair in the "updo" twist she always wore to work. Her white blouse and tailored gray suit were her best. She wanted to look professional and capable.

Unfortunately, at the breakfast table Sybbie decided to fling a handful of smashed bananas in Lila's direction. The mess landed smack on the lapel of her suit. James took one look at Lila's face and tugged her to her feet. "It will come off with a little soap and water," he said firmly. "You'll be good as new. I've got breakfast covered. Go. Finish getting ready."

In the bathroom, Lila stared in the mirror. Who was this

woman she barely recognized? Her eyes were underscored with dark circles and her complexion was pale, too pale.

After successfully removing the splotches of banana, she braced her hands on the sink and bent her head. Deep breaths. Slow and steady. It took five minutes, but at last she achieved a modicum of peace.

With some rosy-cheek blusher and a soft peachy-pink lipstick, she added color to her face. Then she checked her watch. Ten minutes to spare.

In the bedroom, she picked up her purse, briefcase and phone. With one last look around, she went in search of her housemates. In the kitchen, James had tuned the satellite radio to an oldies station and was singing goofy songs to the baby. Sybbie was eating it up, her sleepless night forgotten.

James looked up when Lila entered. His eyes warmed. "You look beautiful, not to mention smart and like a really badass banker."

The reference made her laugh. "I'm not sure that's a thing."

"It will be when they see *you*." He picked up Sybbie. "Give Aunt Lila a kiss, baby girl."

Lila hugged the soft, warm body and felt a wave of love so intense it nearly crippled her resolve. She clung to the baby, even when Sybbie squirmed.

James touched her shoulder. "Go. Everything's going to be fine. You've got this."

Lila, her throat tight, handed him the baby, nodded her head and fled.

James might have underestimated how difficult it was going to be when he volunteered as full-time caregiver for an inquisitive, active infant who was on the cusp of walking. If he turned his back for an instant, Sybbie found something or other she wasn't supposed to have.

It dawned on him that he should have baby-proofed his house before offering his services. That would be first on the agenda this week. And not a minute too soon.

Lila's PDF and extensive notes were helpful for the most part. Unfortunately, when he tried to get the baby to go to sleep at one o'clock, Sybbie did nothing but wail and gnaw on her hand. Clearly the kid hadn't read her own spreadsheet.

He ended up rocking her and letting her chew on a clean, frozen washrag. That tip was compliments of Cassidy, who had given his brother Gavin twins. The thought of multiple babies made James shudder. This parenting stuff was not for the faint of heart.

How had his mother done it all those years ago? Of course, Maeve Kavanagh had been blessed with a lack of financial worry and thus was able to bring in help when she needed it. But still, raising seven boys was an incredible feat. Even more remarkable when you took into account that, by and large, all seven had turned out to be decent, normal human beings.

They'd each had their bumps in the road at one time or another. But his mother was the closest thing to a saint he'd ever met. Even now, one maternal look could bring her grown sons to heel. She was warm and loving and as tough as a drill sergeant.

When Sybbie finally dozed off, James had been planning to make a few phone calls and catch up on email. Instead, he sat down on the couch and went out cold for forty-five minutes. When he woke up, he looked around the room sheepishly, relieved there had been no witnesses.

He could hike for miles and miles in rough terrain and barely get out of breath. But one pint-size kid had brought him to his knees in a matter of hours. His pride took a definite hit.

Fortunately, the rest of the day went smoothly. His

housekeeper came in, so she took care of the kitchen mess and did the laundry. As was her custom, she also prepared a couple of casseroles to put in the freezer for James to use as needed. At his request, she put together a pot of chili and pureed some sweet potatoes in the blender for the baby.

Even with two adults in the house, Sybbie made her presence known. She was pulling up on everything in sight. James followed behind her like a bodyguard, ready at every second to keep her from hurting herself.

He heated one of the casseroles and had it ready at six. But no Lila. He fed Sybbie and played with her until six thirty, but no Lila. He'd texted her at frequent intervals during the day as requested, but had received only a couple of replies.

At seven, he began to worry. At seven thirty, the front door opened. When Lila stepped inside, he was ready to blast her for not letting him know she was okay, but the look on her face stopped him cold. It was defeat, plain and simple. Along with a few other nasty things he couldn't decipher.

"What happened?" he asked, alarmed by her demeanor.

She shrugged. "I'll tell you while I eat, but let's put Sybbie down first."

James winced. "She's already asleep, honey."

"You couldn't wait thirty minutes? I wanted to tuck her in."

"Lila." He tamped down the retort that would only have made things worse. Lila was distraught. His being angry wasn't going to help. "She fell asleep a little before seven. It was all I could do to keep her awake during dinner. She was up a lot last night, remember? The poor thing was comatose. I'm sorry. I know you wanted to say good-night to her, but I didn't have a choice."

Lila pulled herself together visibly. "Of course. I'm

sorry I snapped at you. I'm also beat. I think I'll skip dinner and hit the hay."

He took her briefcase and purse and laid them on the
table in the foyer. "I'm guessing you had a hell of a day.
Why don't you change into comfortable clothes and I'll
heat up some casserole? You need to eat something."

For a moment he thought she was going to fight him.
Then her shoulders rose and fell in a sigh. "Okay. Thanks."

He wondered if she would change her mind, but in fifteen minutes, she returned wearing navy flannel pajama
pants and a pale blue thermal shirt covered in dancing
pink hippos. It was a whimsical design for such a serious woman.

Lila sat down at the table and drank half of the glass
of tea he put in front of her. She managed five or six bites
of the casserole and some salad before shoving her plate
away. With her elbows propped on the table, she buried
her face in her hands.

The nape of her neck struck James as both erotic and
innocent. She had combed out her thick golden hair and
secured it in a messy ponytail. In this attire and without
the formal hairstyle, she looked far younger than her years.

"Tell me what happened, Lila." It was only a hunch on
his part. She might simply be tired from a long day, but
he had a feeling it was more than that.

Lila sat back in her chair and rubbed her eyes like a
little child. When she finally looked at him, he saw the
depth of her disquiet. Now he was getting antsy. "Please
tell me. I'm imagining all kinds of things."

Her smile held no humor. "It was brutal. We never even
got to half the stuff on the list."

"Why not?"

"Several months ago we had to send reams of prelim-
inary paperwork to the auditors. Their job was to comb
through it, make suggestions for improving our informa-

tion streams and then, on-site, they would tackle day-to-day operations."

"And there was a problem with the early paperwork?"

"You might say that. They discovered that one of our valued longtime employees has been embezzling funds."

"Damn."

"Yep. Pretty dreadful."

"But wouldn't earlier audits have turned up something long before now?"

"Well, here's the thing. Helen only began taking money last year, the year covered by the current audit. Turns out, she was very angry when I was brought in from outside for the job of vice president. She thought the position should have been hers."

"Hell, Lila."

"Evidently, she brooded about the perceived injustice for months and months. Then, something snapped I guess, and she convinced herself the money was rightfully hers. All the senior management team, including our district folks and me, had to be in the room when Helen was confronted by the bank examiner. She denied it at first, but she finally broke. In the process, she screamed at me like a fishwife, blaming every bit of her troubles on the 'silly little girl with the bombshell looks who got a promotion based on her smile and her boobs.'"

The last few words came out on a stifled sob.

James was furious. "Someone should have shut her up. There was no reason for you to hear that garbage. You know what she said isn't true."

"Maybe they've all been thinking that."

The look of misery on her face increased his anger. "You're one of the smartest women I know. You've worked long and hard to get where you are in your profession. This Helen person has some mental health issues. You can't blame yourself for any of this." He paused. "How did she take the money, anyway? I can't imagine being able to simply skim the cash drawer."

"No. But it was fairly straightforward and ingenious. Helen handles almost all of our home loans. All she had to do was charge people half a percent more in points on their loans than was actually required. After each loan closed, she altered the paperwork to the correct, lower figures and pocketed the extra cash."

"What if a sharp customer noticed the discrepancy?"

"She claimed it as an honest mistake and fixed it the way it was supposed to be."

Fifteen

Lila regretted trying the casserole. Already it was swimming around in her stomach and making her feel wretched. "I'm sorry. I don't want to eat anymore. But I appreciate everything you did."

James shrugged. "My housekeeper made it. All I had to do was punch a button on the microwave."

She was embarrassed and humiliated and at the end of her rope. "I really do need to go to bed," she muttered.

James stood up. "In a minute. But first, put your head on your arms…on the table. I can see the knots in your neck from here."

"No. It's not—" But she was too late. James had already moved behind her chair. This was becoming a dangerous habit.

He pushed gently on the back of her head. "For once, don't fight me, Lila. Close your eyes. Relax."

When James put his big hands on her upper back, Lila could have wept. It felt so good, and her day had been so bad. She let her mind go blank; concentrated on floating in the ocean. The sun was hot on her skin. The waves held her up, but she undulated in the water as they crested and fell.

James never once did anything that seemed sexual in nature or made her uncomfortable. But this was the man who had long ago made her cry out his name in ragged, gasping climax. For the first time in three years, she let herself admit she still craved his touch.

When she had shared James's bed, he'd had the knack of being able to take her from drowsy pleasure to sharp-edged release in seconds, almost as if he were a magician and her body was a series of silken handkerchiefs being run through his fingers.

Tonight, those memories intruded. As tired as she was, arousal bloomed. Sweet and gentle at first. Then more insistent.

With her eyes still closed and her face buried in her arms, she reached out a hand and captured one of his wrists.

"Am I hurting you?" he asked sharply. "Should I stop?"

In the background, music played. A slow, bluesy jazz number. The kind of thing James had once liked to use in the bedroom to set the mood. She knew such a choice wasn't his intent tonight. The song was random…one of many on the radio.

She sat up slowly, still holding his wrist. When she turned to face him, his face was flushed, his pupils dilated. He had called her the sensible one, but any common sense she possessed had flown out the window, drowned in a rush of yearning and need so deep and wide she had no hope of resisting it…of resisting *him*.

"I want to forget this dreadful day. Help me, James. Make the world go away. For tonight. For old times' sake." She was weak when she needed to be strong, but she was tired of fighting on too many fronts. Here, at least, she could count on the outcome. She could predict and control and plan.

Because what she was asking of James was familiar and amazing and more important at this moment than anything else in the world except little Sybbie.

He drew her to her feet slowly, his eyes searching her face as if suspecting a trap. His suspicion made her ashamed. But not enough to call a halt to the heady rush of anticipation.

"Don't think," she pleaded. "Don't question." She paused, her throat tight. "For the next hour, let's be the us we used to be. Nothing else. No hidden agendas. Just sex. Plain and simple."

James kept his expression impassive. Sex with Lila had never been plain and simple. Nor would it be now. It was messy and heady and completely insane. He'd sworn not to take advantage of her vulnerability. But a man would have to be a saint or a eunuch to turn down such a plea.

He could tell her he would take care of her…that he would make her forget everything, up to and including her name. All of that might be true.

But the real reason he would bow to her wishes was because he was selfish. He wanted, needed, to take her. Wanted it so badly, in fact, that it would be difficult not to hurt her. There was a ravening beast inside him, an animal that hadn't been fed for three long years.

There had been other women in the interim, of course. A handful. But honest to God, he couldn't remember most of their names or faces. None of them had made him half-crazed with hunger. None of them had offered a bliss so rich and deep it bordered on pain.

He'd lost the ability to speak. And after all, what else was there to say?

He didn't try to kiss her. If he did that, he'd have Lila

bent over the kitchen counter before she knew what was happening.

Shaking free of her hold on him, he reversed the position. Now her slender wrist was caught in his firm grip. He pulled her along behind him—through the kitchen door, down the hall, into her bedroom.

Sybbie's door was closed. Lila stopped him only once. "The baby monitor?" she asked in a whisper.

"In my pocket." He took it out and set it on the dresser. For thirty seconds, maybe a minute, he and Lila stood side by side and looked at the sleeping child. Sybbie was not restless tonight. At least not yet. She dozed peacefully, her tiny fist curled against her mouth.

Lila turned to him. "I want you, James."

In her sock feet, she seemed small to him, infinitely fragile. Carefully, he freed the band from her ponytail and tossed the elastic aside. "Let me brush your hair," he said.

Her eyes widened, but she nodded. In his guest room was an old-fashioned vanity with a matching stool and age-spotted mirror. The beautiful antique set was a gift from his mother when he first bought the house and renovated it. She'd claimed it came over on the boat from Ireland, though that might have been a whimsical exaggeration on her part.

James led Lila across the room and made her sit. Carefully, he lifted the hem of her blue pajama top and pulled it up over her head. When he was finished, Lila's reflection in the mirror resembled that of a nude he'd seen in a museum once upon a time. Her dark eyes were wary.

"Hand me the brush." The words came out guttural and demanding, even to his own ears. Lila didn't like his bossiness, as a rule. Tonight, she didn't protest.

There was only one other seat in the room, a small chintz-covered armchair that looked far too delicate for his big frame. But it was the perfect height to sit behind Lila and be able to watch her in the mirror while he wielded the brush.

He'd be hard-pressed to say which was softer, Lila's silky blond hair or her creamy skin. Slowly he ran the brush from her crown down through thick waves to her back. Every time his fingers brushed her bare skin, he saw her flinch.

"You're the most beautiful thing I've ever seen," he said, entirely sincere. "The body of an angel and the sharp tongue of the devil's mistress. But I wouldn't have it any differently. In a weird, twisted sort of way, I always enjoyed our fights. Except for the times you cried. Those tore me apart."

Lila's tongue wet her lips. He saw the muscles in her throat work when she swallowed. "You wanted an amenable, biddable girlfriend," she whispered. "One who would agree with everything you said."

"I was an idiot." He knew that now.

"Hey," she said. "At last, something I can agree with." The laughter in her eyes made him feel ten feet tall. He would walk through cut glass to erase the pain he'd witnessed on her face when she finally came home tonight.

"Shrew," he teased.

"Neanderthal." She leaned back against him and sighed.

It was an old game they played…one that often ended up between the sheets. His body hummed with desire, every inch of his skin and flesh and bones taut with anticipation. The brush tumbled to the floor, his fingers slack, his sex rigid and aching.

He put his arms around her and touched her dark pink nipples. They were hard and puckered. Lila sucked in a sharp breath when he tugged at them. In the mirror, his tanned fingers were in stark contrast to her ivory breasts.

Mesmerized by the sensual image, he cupped and plumped the full, ripe curves.

Lila's eyelids fluttered shut.

"Look at me," he said sharply. "Look at us."

She was startled, trembling with arousal. He wanted to draw out the playful prelude for hours. Until the night waned and dawn tinted the sky with pink, the same rosy color as Lila's lips.

"Stand up," he said. "I want to see all of you."

He kept waiting for Lila to push back, to demand an equal share. But tonight, it seemed, her submission was going to be a gift to them both. The thought of an acquiescent Lila made him shake. He adored matching wits with her, battling for supremacy in the bedroom.

They had never played these roles before. Was her passive pleasure all she had left to give after a long, hard day? Or was she doing this deliberately to drive him slowly out of his mind?

Did it matter?

When she was on her feet, he pushed the stool aside. Now he drew her backward two steps, positioning her in the vee of his thighs. He ran his hands from her narrow waist, down over curvy hips, to her knees. Pressing a kiss to the bottom of her spine, or at least as far as he could reach, he sank his fingers into soft flannel and began dragging Lila's last bit of clothing down her legs.

For a moment, she tightened her thighs instinctively, but he was having none of that. "Move your feet apart," he croaked. "I want all of you at my fingertips."

She tried, but stumbled, hampered by the fabric binding her limbs. After steadying her with one hand, he finished his job, drawing the garment over one foot at a time and baring her completely.

When he had met his goal, he stopped. It was hard to

breathe, hard to think. Why had he never paused to pay homage to Lila's incredible body? She thought she was too fat. He knew she was perfect. Her curves were intensely feminine, the stuff of male fantasy.

He rested his cheek against the side of her hip, his gaze fixed on the reflection of his hands exploring Lila's body. He could have busied himself above the waist for hours, but he was eager to indulge darker needs.

The triangle of perfection between her thighs beckoned a man's questing fingertip. His Lila was clean shaven but for the tiniest triangle of golden fluff. She shuddered and groaned when he delved into her moist, quivering flesh. He sensed she was already dangerously close to the peak. Hell, so was he.

He was torn between conflicting desires. The animal inside him wanted hard and fast and reckless. The older, wiser James needed to savor every drop of an experience that was very possibly never to be repeated.

That thought made him angry and morose, so he locked it away.

"Shall I make you come, my tart, sweet Lila?"

A tiny frown appeared between her eyebrows. "Not without you inside me."

"Is that rebellion I hear? Are you challenging my authority?" He injected a note of steel into the query and was rewarded for his efforts when Lila's mouth dropped open.

"Um, no…" she said hesitantly.

"So you won't stop me if I make you climax?"

The blunt question turned her face red. She shook her head in a negative, clearly unable to speak.

"That's my girl," he crooned.

Ruthlessly, he probed deeper with two fingers, stroking the tiny spot that controlled every zing of pleasure.

Lila's eyes were closed now, squeezed shut in fact, her

chest heaving, her voluptuous breasts rising and falling in a way that almost distracted him from his mission.

He focused on the task at hand. "Come for me, lovely Lila. Let go. Give in. I'm going to make you fly."

Sixteen

Lila felt the rush of orgasm and barely managed to stop it. Trapped between James's arms and legs, she was terrified she might lose every bit of herself and never get it back.

He was so close, pressed as he was against her bare bottom, that he inevitably recognized her momentary resistance. He froze. "I'll stop, my Lila, but only if you command me. Is that what you want?"

His fingers were still inside her, the heel of his hand pressed firmly against her mound. She felt as if he possessed her completely, and yet the wicked man was still fully clothed. "Yes. No. I don't know. Do what you will, James. I can't make the decisions tonight. I don't want to."

She saw him frown, registered the tension in his big frame. "That's a dangerous path to walk."

Her eyes met his in the mirror. "I trust you."

James's expression was transfixed. For a moment, she could swear his gaze went blind, though his eyes were open wide. He never moved; not a breath, not an involuntary flexing of muscle.

"Did I say something wrong?" she asked, troubled.

He shook his head as if to clear it. "No. Quite the contrary. But since apparently I'm calling the shots tonight, you might as well keep quiet from here on out. Or do I need to gag you?"

"You can't be serious."

"Try me."

James had taken her at her word. He was in control. And liking it. She shivered hard, her body flooded with enough adrenaline and sexual heat to vaporize every bit of oxygen in the room.

She wanted to say she understood…that for once, she wouldn't argue. But if she said it out loud, he might get some kinky idea about punishing her, and she wasn't quite ready for that.

Instead, she stood docilely, her head bowed, her gaze on the tiny pattern in the rug. Pale pink baby rosebuds twining in a garland of navy and green. For as long as she lived, that image would be burned into her retinas. Because when James went back to his program of benign torture, she very nearly lost her mind.

The independent feminist part of her was aghast that she had surrendered so easily. But the aching, hungry, sex-starved woman who also inhabited her body reveled in the touch of a firm masculine hand.

James bent and bit the fleshy curve of her ass. "Let's start with one and see how far we can go."

One what? she wondered, dazed. The answer wasn't difficult to decipher. He spread her legs another three inches, stroked her firmly and held her as she cried out and shattered in his embrace.

There are times a woman wonders about her own capacity for pleasure. Tonight tested those limits. She was still trembling after the first orgasm, when James scooped her up and dumped her on the bed. Not too much finesse, but plenty of raw masculine determination.

Before she could gather her wits, he was between her legs, his mouth pressed to her quivering sex. "No," she cried. "Not so soon. I can't stand it."

Her vocal protest drew swift retribution. He had her over his lap in seconds. When he landed a blow with a firm hand on her bottom, she winced. But her body was not as evolved as her intellect. The naughty swat on her behind sent her spiraling upward again.

James caressed the stinging flesh. "Are you ready to do as I say?"

Upside down and breathless, she nodded. Despite her position, even though blood rushed to her head, there was plenty left to keep the rest of her from being numb. When he righted her, she transgressed again. On purpose. "Take your clothes off, James. Please. I want to touch you."

His eyebrows rose and his nostrils flared. "Are you *asking* for a spanking?"

"Maybe later," she muttered, her fingers struggling with his belt buckle. "Besides, you like it when I'm noisy."

His sly grin made her heart thump faster. "You've got me there."

Maybe the spectacular orgasm had made her clumsy, or maybe she was too wiped out to concentrate, but she had the hardest time getting him undressed. James just laughed at her, his arms dangling at his sides.

"James Buchanan Kavanagh," she hissed. "Help me."

"All you had to do was ask."

His smart-aleck rejoinder was way too smug. The man clearly enjoyed having her panting and breathless, tearing at his shirt like a crazed groupie. "You are not a nice person," she stated categorically.

James, not bothering to refute her accusation, stepped

out of his pants, socks and shoes and stripped off his boxers.

Lila blinked. Was he even better-looking than he had been three years ago? Or was she being seduced by his blinding grin and sexy, bad-boy attitude? He was completely nude now except for the shirt that hung open, hiding nothing of his flat belly and broad, hair-dusted chest.

Oh, my.

James held out his arms. "What next?"

"You're in charge, remember?"

He chuckled. "You seem to have a little difficulty with that concept. Don't get me wrong. I like a woman who knows what she wants."

"I tried being quiet and retiring when I was a teenager. It didn't get me far."

"So what you're saying is, if I want to silence you, I'm going to need that gag, after all."

"Or you could kiss me."

She meant it to sound like a joke…a dare. But it didn't come out that way at all. If James was paying attention, there was no way he could miss her needy, breathless adoration. It should have embarrassed her. Letting him see how much she wanted him gave him an advantage in their battle of the sexes.

But if anything, her plea destroyed James's cocky confidence. Keeping his gaze locked on hers, he removed the shirt and held out a hand. "Lila Baxter, will you do me the honor of going to bed with me?"

They climbed onto her mattress in tandem, all arms and legs and poking elbows. He tried to pull back the covers. She tried to help. They would probably have given up and stayed on top if the room hadn't been a smidgen uncomfortable. She'd left her window partially open during the day, and now the air was freezing.

At last they found themselves together, face-to-face, sharing the same breathless bubble of intimacy.

He traced her eyebrows with one finger and kissed her nose. "I've missed you, Lila."

The raw honesty deserved an equal measure in return. She took a deep breath, barely able to meet his eyes. It hurt too much. "I was heartbroken when we ended things," she whispered. "But I spent too much of my life in a household filled with conflict. I didn't want to end up like one of those old couples who snipe and gripe at each other constantly."

"Our arguments were different," he insisted.

"How so?"

"We only argued because we couldn't have sex 24/7."

"Ah. That's your explanation?"

He cupped the nearest breast and squeezed lightly. "It was either that or the fact that you couldn't admit I was right ninety-nine percent of the time."

She rolled her eyes. "It's coming back to me now. Arrogant. Bossy. Opinionated."

He kissed her sweetly. "Don't be so hard on yourself, honey."

The droll humor was a revelation. If she weren't mistaken, James rued their contentious past as much as she did. "People don't really change."

"Who says so?"

She shrugged, noticing the way his interesting man parts were nudging her lower belly. "Everyone. The internet."

"Well, then, it must be true."

Skating around the subject of their relationship, past or present, made her uneasy. Sex was easier. Less volatile, oddly enough.

She nibbled his collarbone and slipped one hand beneath the sheet to find the hard, smooth length of him.

"You promised me lots of orgasms." It had been so long since they had been this close. So very long.

"Don't be in such a hurry, Lila. Good things come to those who wait."

"Said no man, ever. How much longer do you think you can resist me?"

He nuzzled her neck. "Do the people at that stuffy bank know what a firecracker you are?"

"I don't want to talk about my job. Unless you want to kill the mood entirely."

"Fair point." Every vestige of humor left his face. He cupped her cheek. "But I'm sorry you've had to juggle so much lately." His piercing gaze stripped her bare emotionally. It was not a comfortable feeling.

She nodded jerkily. "I have to look at the big picture, though. Other people's lives are much worse."

"That doesn't minimize *your* struggles."

"Tell me what to do, James." This close, he couldn't see her face. Her nose was buried in his shoulder. But she felt him tense.

"I can't do that, Lila. I'll support you and help you, but this is your decision."

Tears burned her eyes. "Three years ago, you couldn't keep your nose out of my business. Where's that irritating, overbearing guy now?"

"Maybe he's learned a thing or two."

"Make love to me, James. It's late, and I have a sweet little responsibility who doesn't care when I get to bed."

He rolled on top of her, but spared her his weight by bracing his arms on either side of her head. "You should know that I planted termites at your house so I could lure you into my trap."

She gaped at him and then burst out laughing. "No, you did not."

He shrugged, his smile rueful. "I might have…if I had thought of it. I wanted you in my bed again."

That sobered her, though she kept her smile in place. In his bed. Not in his life. It was a fine distinction but an important one. Curling her arms around his neck, she pulled him down for a teasing kiss. "Please tell me you have protection."

He nodded. "In my pocket every day since you walked over here and asked for my help."

"I like a man who's prepared. But I might point out that your pants are on the floor."

The expression on his face was priceless. "Damn. Give me ten seconds."

It was closer to twenty, but she was in a generous mood. When he pushed inside her with a groan that rumbled against her chest, she knew she had made a mistake. She should have stayed far away from James Kavanagh. Because she was about to get her heart broken all over again.

Seventeen

James surfaced slowly, disoriented and confused. Some sound had awoken him. He eased from Lila's embrace and reached for the baby monitor. Sybbie was stirring. According to the clock, it was only 3:00 a.m. Surely she would go back to sleep.

When the baby settled without further movement, he breathed a sigh of relief. He turned on his side and studied Lila's sleeping face. Last night had been a revelation. The sex was amazing—that part hadn't changed. But the stakes were higher, far higher than they had been three years ago. He was in deep, maybe too deep. He'd let Lila's situation with Sybbie involve him emotionally. And that was a recipe for disaster. Because he was pretty sure his beautiful, passionate lover was convinced she had to give the baby away.

Because he had sworn to her that he had changed, he couldn't in all good conscience pressure her into the decision *he* thought was best. What happened next was up to Lila entirely.

In the midst of his soul-searching, she roused, scraping the hair from her face and yawning. "What's wrong?"

He pulled her against him, spooning her back. "Nothing. Go back to sleep."

But Lila never had been the kind to sleep easily. She sat up, holding the sheet to her breasts. "What time is it?"

"Late." He tugged on her arm. "C'mon. Close your eyes."

He could almost feel the doubts and regret washing over her. "God, James, what did I do?"

"*You* didn't do anything. *We* had sex. And it was pretty damned awesome. In fact, now that you're awake, I'd be happy to try again."

When he tried a second time to drag her back into the warm cocoon of covers, she scooted away from him. "This was a mistake."

"Lord give me strength."

Her hands were white-knuckled on the bedsheet…as if that thin piece of cotton fabric could protect her. "I know I started this," she said. "So I have to take responsibility. I shouldn't have reached out to you. I was upset, but that's no excuse. Please go."

He almost wanted her to lay the situation at his door, so they could yell at each other. Lila's stoic acceptance of blame, along with her clear misery, gave him a hollow feeling in his gut.

"Lila," he said, summoning every bit of understanding and concern he could muster. "Everything's the same. We're still friends. Don't panic over nothing."

"So sex with me was nothing?" He hadn't thought she could look any more hurt or shattered. But apparently, he was doomed to say the wrong thing. Now that he thought about it, that was the theme of their relationship.

Suddenly, he was over it. Lila was kicking him out of

his own damned guest room. Fine. If that's the way she wanted it.

He tumbled out of bed and dragged on his pants, sans underwear. His hands were shaking he was so angry. Why did it always have to be like this between them? Why couldn't they ever have a relationship that was simple and easy? "I will show up at eight every morning as I promised. But I'm going to spend the evenings at your place until I get the renovation finished. You'll be back in your own bed by Friday, so help me God. And the next time you think about asking somebody for help, my door is closed, locked and bolted from the inside."

"Where are you going?" she cried.

"Anywhere you're not. Thanks for nothing, sweetheart. The sooner you and I are back to being next-door enemies, the better."

He wanted to slam things and storm out of the house, but even in the midst of his fury, he wouldn't wake the baby. After grabbing a few personal necessities from his bedroom, he tiptoed downstairs and departed the premises like a thief in the night.

His body should have been sated and lax. Sex with Lila had been better than ever. Somehow, it wasn't enough. He wanted more. He wanted her to trust him. To rely on him.

Did he have a savior complex? Was his constant need to fix things some kind of deep-seated personality flaw?

With the key to Lila's house in his hand, he crossed the side yard and let himself in. He hadn't even had a chance to tell her that the pest control guys had been there all day. And that her property had been given the all clear.

Tonight, he would get back to the simple renovation she had requested. He wanted to finish it quickly so he could close the book on this disturbing chapter of his life. For now, though, he needed a couple of hours' sleep.

Upstairs, Lila's bed would be comfortable and warm. But he couldn't bring himself to invade her private space. Instead, he plopped down on her not-quite-long-enough sofa, kicked off his shoes and closed his eyes.

He must have slept. He knew he had. Still, when the alarm on his phone went off some time later, he groaned and cursed. Every bone in his body ached. Even worse, he woke up hard, because he'd been dreaming about sex. With she-who-must-not-be-named. From this moment forward, he and Lila were history. This time, it was going to stick.

After splashing water on his face, he went back to face the music. At least Sybbie was happy to see him. Her aunt could barely look him in the eye. Lila was dressed for work. Even carefully applied cosmetics couldn't hide the effects of a sleepless night.

They barely spoke a dozen words to each other. Only the absolute minimum necessary information concerning the child. The baby, thank God, was too young to pick up on undercurrents. She had no clue that the adults were at odds.

When Lila walked out of the kitchen and a few moments later closed the front door, James reached for the bottle of ibuprofen he kept in the cabinet beside the refrigerator. Today was going to test his limits as a human being. All he wanted to do was sleep.

As soon as he had the renovation completed—hopefully Thursday night—he had to get out of town and clear his head. He was a mess. The fact that Sybbie had already wormed her way into his heart told him there would be hard days ahead. He couldn't *make* Lila keep the child, and he sure as hell didn't want a front-row seat if the worst happened.

Lila hadn't thought her days could get much more difficult, but she was wrong. Even though the remainder of the audit ran smoothly, things were unsettled at the bank. Helen, flanked by an armed guard, had been compelled to clean out her desk and exit the premises, metaphorical pink slip in hand.

She had been a popular employee and a friend to many. Lila wasn't sure if it was her imagination or not, but it seemed as if people had drawn lines in the sand, with most of them on Helen's side.

Lila didn't know what to say, so she kept her mouth shut. The tension headache she battled seemed to have moved in for the duration.

Thursday, she had to have a break. She called Mia and begged her to come downtown for a meal. The audit had required extra hours. It wouldn't hurt to take a long lunch today.

Over quiche and fruit salad, the two women talked of inconsequential topics. But when their food was served and the waitress left them in peace, Mia jumped in without invitation.

"No offense, hon," she said, "but you look like hell."

"With friends like you who needs enemies? It's been a tough week."

"So I hear. According to Dylan, you and James had a fight to end all fights. Dylan says James is pissed. I swear I don't understand why the two of you can't get along."

Lila winced, taking a swallow of tea to ease the lump in her throat. "It's complicated, and it's personal."

"Fair enough. But that doesn't explain why you called and invited me to lunch sounding like you were about to jump off a bridge."

"Don't make jokes about suicide. It's insensitive."

"Fine. Then explain yourself, woman."

Lila realized she had no clue how to do that, though she had to try. "I need to decide whether I'm going to keep Sybbie or give her up for adoption. James offered to look after her for a couple of months so I wouldn't make any snap decisions, but…"

"But what?"

"I realized this week that the longer I keep her, the harder it will be for her and for me to say goodbye later. She's already lost her mother and her father. If I'm not going to be the one to love her and raise her, I should figure that out now…before she gets too attached to me."

Mia shook her head, her expression compassionate. "Here's the thing, Lila. You have an analytical mind. I understand, because that's how I operate. When I decided to have a baby on my own, I thought I had every single detail figured out. But I didn't. I had a high-paying job working in a state-of-the-art biotech lab. My IQ was impressive. I'd never really failed at anything. Parenthood was something entirely different, though."

"Things turned out all right. Clearly."

"But not before I had a breakdown. Here's the hard truth. People who tell you it's possible to have it all are full of crap. Bringing a child into the world, however it happens, means sacrifice and compromise…period."

"So what are you saying?"

"Do you like your job, Lila?"

No one had ever asked her that. "I'm good at it. I've worked hard for promotions and more responsibility. I make a more-than-decent living."

"Then adopt Sybbie, if that's what you want, and put her in day care while you're at work. People all over the modern world do that, and their kids turn out to be bright, well-adjusted human beings."

"I know. I'm sure I could cobble together child care until she turns twelve months. Then I can enroll her in a proper day care."

"So what's stopping you? Do you not want to have babies at all? Or is it that Sybbie isn't your biological child?"

"No," Lila said sharply. "It's not that. I adore her."

Mia frowned. "I don't see the problem."

Lila fiddled with her dessert spoon. The Kavanaghs, even the in-laws, all seemed to be successful and have their lives in perfect working order. Her friend surely wouldn't understand Lila's doubts.

Mia reached across the table. "Talk to me, sweetie. I can see the wheels turning, but I'm not getting the whole picture."

Oh, what the hell. This week had done a number on Lila's pride and self-esteem. She might as well be up-front. "I'm scared I don't have what it takes to be a good mother," she said, the words flat. "Actually, I'm scared to be a parent, period. The thought of being responsible for another human life terrifies me. The reason I've thrown myself into my career so wholeheartedly is because I convinced myself a long time ago I didn't want children. Because of that choice, I knew I needed something in my life that mattered…something to fill the void. I know I'm good at what I do. When I'm at work I feel capable and in control."

Mia's expression was sober. "And now?"

Lila waved a hand. "I've fallen in love with my niece. Even so, the thought of adopting her makes me literally sick with fear. My banking job is concrete and dependable. Numbers don't change. I know how to keep track of them. If I give up my career, or even if I keep it and try to put Sybbie's needs first, there's a real possibility I could fail at both."

"Okay. I can understand that."

"Aside from being petrified to be her mom, I think Sybbie should have a daddy, too. With a swing set in the yard and a station wagon parked in the driveway."

"Do auto companies even make station wagons anymore?" Mia teased.

"You know what I mean. I never imagined I'd be a single parent."

"And that's why you want to give her up?"

"I don't *want* to give her up. I want what's best for everyone involved."

"And where does James come into all this?"

The blunt question took her breath. "Um…"

Mia took pity on her. "Never mind. That's between you two. But I happen to know the guy likes kids."

"You think I should marry a sugar daddy and let him take care of me?"

Mia's eyes flashed. "The Kavanaghs are loaded, but that's not why I married Dylan. I love him. Period."

"I know. I'm sorry. That came out wrong."

"James was on the right track when he encouraged you not to make any hasty decisions. What you choose to do now will stay with you the rest of your life…right or wrong…good or bad."

"You'd make a lousy cheerleader."

"Trust me," Mia said, shuddering. "I didn't even come close. My high school years were dismal. But that's a story for another day." She sighed and sat back in her chair. "I don't know what you wanted from me, but I feel like I've failed."

"It's my problem." Lila grimaced. "I suppose I was hoping you'd tip the scales one way or another, but that's not fair to either of us."

"No. And it wouldn't have served you well in the end. We're all different, Lila. Your sister. You. Me. There's no one-woman-fits-all role. You have to dig deep and find your answer in your own backyard."

"Oh. So now we're doing *Wizard of Oz*?"

"There are a lot of good life lessons in that movie."

"Yes. I suppose. But where are the flying monkeys when you need one?"

* * *

Mia had given Lila a lot to think about. Every time Lila felt sure she was going to keep Sybbie and raise her as her own daughter, the reality of the situation reared its ugly head. The choices were clear-cut. Either give the baby up for adoption...or keep her and face her worst fears.

Sybbie was heartbreakingly vulnerable. So much could go wrong. Already, the baby had lost her parents and everything she had known and loved during her short life. Surely she deserved a mother who wasn't terrified to be a parent.

Lila and James had both experienced abandonment as children, though in vastly different ways. It didn't take a genius to see that James thought she should keep Sybbie. But he wasn't volunteering to be the daddy.

The questions went round and round in Lila's head until she wanted to scream or pitch a fit or *something* to ease the tension that was her constant companion. But gradually, she found a tenuous sense of peace. She knew what she had to do.

Friday, when she got home from work, James met her at the door with Sybbie on his hip. The baby gave her a slobbery smile and held out her arms. James was stone-faced.

He put his hands in his back pockets after Lila took the baby from him. "The work at your house is done," he said bluntly. "I've asked Dylan to help you move the baby bed back to where it belongs after dinner."

"Where will you be?" she asked, annoyed that he was passing her off to his brother.

"I'm getting out of town for a few days."

"I see."

"I doubt you do, Lila. You're too stubborn to see anything beyond the tip of your nose."

He stopped and held up both hands. "I told myself I wasn't going to do that. Arguing will get us nowhere."

His cold manner and distant expression cut her to the bone. "I have news, as well," she said impulsively. "I've made a decision about Sybbie. I won't be needing your babysitting services anymore after today."

Shock flashed across his face followed in quick succession by anger and something else that looked a lot like pain. He inhaled sharply. "Whatever you say, Lila. You just can't stomach taking help from me, can you? You have to do it all on your own. Well, don't expect me to come running the next time you're in trouble. I've done my share. I'm through."

As she watched, her world in ashes, James walked out of the house and out of her life.

The rest of the day was almost anticlimactic. Dylan showed up as promised just after Lila finished feeding Sybbie. He disassembled the baby bed, carried the pieces across the side yard and put everything back together in the brand-new nursery James had created out of her old dining room. Now she and Sybbie would both be comfortable on the main floor.

Not only had James finished the structural changes, but he had painted the new walls and, as far as she could tell, cleaned up every speck of debris. Her new arrangement was perfect.

When Sybbie was asleep, Lila tucked the baby monitor in her pocket and made three trips back and forth across the lawn to retrieve her personal belongings. When she had erased every mark of her presence in James's home, she carefully locked his front door and shoved the key through the mail slot.

Then she went home, showered, climbed into her own bed and cried herself to sleep.

Eighteen

James was cold to the bone after his confrontation with Lila, despite the warm autumn afternoon. Apparently, nothing he could say would sway her. She was giving Sybbie up for adoption. His offer to buy her some time, to free her from the worry of child care, had lasted a paltry five days.

He should have known better than to get attached to the kid. He would lay down his life for any of his nieces and nephews. They looked at him as a human jungle gym, and he loved it. Even the thought of one of them being seriously ill scared him to death. He didn't know how parents did it.

The only way to escape the bitter disappointment was to get away from Lila...and from civilization in general. Saturday morning, he made his preparations. His overnight pack was familiar and worn. He could load it successfully in half an hour, including a tent and sleeping bag.

By lunchtime, he was good to go.

Because he kept dehydrated meals on hand, all he needed to grab from the bowl on his kitchen table were some apples and oranges. After that, he jumped into the old beat-up Jeep he used for his explorations and drove it into the woods as far as the road went. Then he got out and walked.

It was a gorgeous late September day. Silver Glen, mountain valley that it was, sat at an altitude of three thousand feet. Here, the leaves were already exploding into gold and reds and oranges.

Normally, such an excursion cleared his mind as soon as his feet hit the trail. But that wasn't going to happen today. Today, he would have to outrun his demons. His pack weighed fifty pounds, but he barely noticed. He was not a fan of gyms. This was how he got his exercise.

After five miles of hard, steady walking, he found the small clearing he sometimes used as a campsite. The stack of firewood he had collected the last time he visited was still there. Soon, he had a fire blazing and water boiling for coffee.

He poured a measure of water into the small tin pot he carried, added the package of beef and vegetables and propped the metal container over the coals. The stew would do nicely for an evening meal.

As he ate, he tried to center himself. He did everything to empty his mind and regain a sense of peace. But anger still hummed in his veins. Or at least he was going to call it anger. A man didn't want to admit certain things, even to himself.

In his bank account and among all of his various financial holdings, he had enough money to travel anywhere in the world—to buy a yacht; to build a dream house of any size and shape; to shower a woman with diamonds and fancy clothes; hell, he could even sign up to be the next passenger on a space voyage if he chose. Despite the freedom those assets represented, the money had never meant much to him.

Maybe that sounded like poor-little-rich-boy, but it was the truth. The Kavanaghs were financially stable, because one of their ancestors had discovered a silver mine at a time when that was a big deal. Every subsequent generation had worked hard and increased the bottom line.

But that same silver mine had robbed James—robbed him of the chance to play catch with his dad, to enter a Scouting event for father/son teams, to go to NFL games and to learn how to drive and a million other things.

He'd had his oldest brothers to look up to, of course. Liam was a rock, and Dylan was always in his corner. But the "dad' thing was a festering wound that never seemed to heal no matter how many times he covered it in Band-Aids.

His mother had survived the loss of her spouse. All his siblings seemed perfectly well-adjusted, despite what had happened years ago. Why was James the only one screwed up when he didn't even remember the man?

At eight o'clock, he separated the coals of the fire and strung his pack up in a tree so as not to attract bears. The night was cold, but his sleeping bag was rated for twenty below. Once he zipped the tent and crawled inside the cocoon, he was snug and warm. Still, sleep didn't come.

He lay awake for hours listening to the familiar sounds of the forest. The dark night held no fears for him. He knew how to handle himself in almost any situation, either with his wits or his physical strength.

What he didn't know was why he was drawn to a woman who was so clearly wrong for him.

When he finally dozed off, he dreamed. Unsettling, disjointed images of Sybbie and Lila and a man with no face. He kept trying to save all three, but a giant rift opened up and swallowed them, leaving James alone on the edge of the abyss.

At dawn, he gave up and climbed out to meet the new day. He wished it had been raining. A dull, drenching downpour of a morning would have suited his mood. Instead, the sun rose, brilliant and warm…the birds sang… and the coffee was just the way he liked it.

Even in the midst of his pity party, he had to smile. Maybe someone was trying to send him a message. *Man up, Kavanagh, and quit being such an a-hole.*

Despite his unsettled night, he began to come out of his funk. He was a Kavanagh, but that didn't mean everything in life was going to go his way. The first thing he needed to do was find a new house to renovate…one he could live in while he did the work. Because he wasn't a masochist. He needed to move across town from Lila, sooner rather than later.

Today he left his heavy pack at the campsite, so he was able to walk faster and harder. He pushed himself on and on. By the time midafternoon rolled around, he had reached a part of the far end of the mountain where he rarely explored. The trails were rocky and difficult, and there were no views to reward a determined hiker.

At one point, he came to a deep ravine. Initially, it had been caused by a landslide. Now every time there were heavy spring rains, the gash in the earth became an impromptu waterfall.

Today, though, it was September. The mountain was dry. And the ragged slice was the perfect way to challenge his aching body. He scuttled down the drop-off all the way to the bottom. Then he scrabbled his way to the top of the other side, all his muscles screaming.

When he was finished, he did it again, just for the hell of it. Maybe if he was exhausted enough tonight, he'd be able to sleep.

Sadly, he'd never been the kind of guy who knew when to quit. On his third attempt, he sliced his hand on a rock. The sharp pain shocked him so much, he lost his precarious balance and tumbled in a free fall. The only thing that ultimately stopped his descent was slamming into a broad ridge of rock.

He lay there, breathless, and waited for the world to quit spinning. He had his cell phone for emergencies, but he was deep in the ravine, so reception would be iffy. Still, he could probably climb back up. As soon as he had rested for a few minutes.

At last he got to his feet, moving gingerly and cataloguing his bumps and bruises. He'd be sore as hell tomorrow, but he could find no lasting damage.

The rock on which he stood was part of harder strata than the surrounding crumbly sandstone. His perch was in no danger of disintegrating. That said, the sun was getting low in the sky, casting deep shadows where he paused to evaluate the situation.

The sturdy ledge was large enough that several intrepid bushes had taken root. Perhaps he could snap off part of one and use it as a climbing tool. As he bent to examine the foliage, a recess in the rock caught his eye, a place where a second, smaller ledge extended over part of the one that had broken his fall.

Something white lay in the dust. He took two steps forward. The ledge was firm. This wasn't a cave where he might confront some kind of dangerous creature. It was barely enough of an indentation to shelter a man from a sudden thunderstorm if need be.

When he bent to examine the debris, he jumped back, cursing in shock, unable to process what he was seeing. He hunched over and lost the contents of his stomach. It couldn't be. Not after all this time.

With shaking hands, he grabbed his water bottle and took a long swig. His forehead was damp with perspiration, but he felt cold and shivery. Steeling himself, he moved closer to the far end of the ledge and looked again.

The stark truth registered. What had first appeared to be sun-bleached pieces of wood was actually a skeleton.

All sorts of thoughts spun in his brain. This wasn't his father. It was the remains of an unlucky hiker. Or some old person who had come to the mountains to die.

In his heart, he knew the truth, but he rejected it. It was too painful, too wretchedly sad.

He squatted in silence until his thighs and knees screamed with discomfort. Should he touch it? All the crime shows he had ever watched came back to him. The police needed to be notified. Then James could abdicate the responsibility for this gruesome discovery and place it in their capable hands.

Any of the victim's clothing had long since rotted away. James took a deep cleansing breath and moved even closer, determined not to be at the mercy of his emotions. The Kavanagh family had combed through all the unresolved missing person reports in the last thirty years. Other than Reggie Kavanagh, there were only three remaining. One had drowned. One was a suspected suicide. And one involved an airplane crash.

None of those scenarios matched this location.

In the end, there was no doubt. Deep in a corner of the cramped space, James saw something shiny. Being careful not to touch the bones, he reached for the almost-hidden item and caught it as it rolled free. A gold wedding ring. With an inscription. The symbol of everlasting love and union that Maeve Kavanagh had given her new husband almost four decades ago.

Clutching the ring in his hand, James backed away carefully and stood up. Oddly, he felt nothing. He had enough presence of mind to wonder if he was in shock. There was no longer any doubt about what had happened to Reggie Kavanagh. James's quest was over.

His legs felt funny. He had to sit down on his butt and suck great gasps of air for a good five minutes before he could move again. After that, he slipped the ring into a zippered pocket and then went hell-for-leather up the steep-walled ravine as if all the hounds of the underworld were at his heels.

At the top, he barely stopped to breathe. He ran, not walked, back the way he had come, risking a broken ankle on the tangled trail. But he had to get to high ground. It was the only way to find a strong cell signal.

When he reached a familiar spot, he pulled out his phone with trembling hands and dialed the police. In halting words, he told the tale as briefly and succinctly as he could. Given the evidence he had found—the solid gold wedding band—and the remoteness of the location, the authorities gave permission for the remains to be removed.

Then, feeling no less unsettled than he had before, James called his brother Patrick. Patrick was next up the line, only two years older than James. Not only that, but Patrick was the only other sibling who knew these mountains as well as James.

Patrick's company, Silver Reflections, offered respite for stressed-out execs of Fortune 500 companies. He also ran "survival" camps and team-building events for those same kinds of companies.

Fortunately, Patrick answered on the second ring. "What's up, little bro?"

"I need you to meet me on the ridge above the giant boulder...where we used to bring girls to make out."

"Now? I'm supposed to be taking Libby to dinner tonight."

"This is important. She'll understand, I swear."

Patrick's voice sharpened. "Are you hurt?"

"No. I'm fine." James took a deep ragged breath. "But I need you to come. As soon as you can. I'll wait."

* * *

James was prepared to spend the night on the bare ground if need be. He couldn't go back after seeing what he had seen, but he didn't know how long it would take his sibling to get on the trail.

Patrick must have recognized the unaccustomed urgency in his brother's voice. He showed up barely two hours after James called him. "What now?" he asked, his expression troubled.

James wiped a hand over his face. "I wasn't thinking clearly. It's almost dark. I should have let you wait until tomorrow morning."

Patrick sat on a rock and pulled out his water. After a long drink, he capped the plastic pouch and frowned. "I've never seen you like this. You're scaring me. The James I know is a man of steel. In every situation. What in the hell is going on?"

James's stomach twisted again in a spasm of nausea. He stared at the waning sun, trying to get warm. "I found our father's body."

Nineteen

In the end, it made sense to go back to the campsite. The tent, the food, everything they needed was there. While they still had a signal, Patrick called Libby and told her what was going on. But he warned her not to say anything to anybody. There was no sense in upsetting people earlier than necessary.

After a cobbled-together meal, James unzipped his sleeping bag and opened it flat. They fell on top of it and were asleep almost instantly.

At first light they swallowed coffee, ate an orange each and walked back out along the lonesome ridge. James's heart raced a thousand miles an hour, though their pace was not strenuous.

Maybe he'd imagined the whole thing. After all, he'd taken a hard fall. He might have been momentarily confused. When he said as much, Patrick stopped and stared at him. "Do you really believe that?"

James swallowed. "No."

"Then let's keep going."

When they arrived at the ravine, they faced their first quandary. James had landed on the ledge by accident. Actually trying to access it on purpose would be far more difficult.

Patrick's frown was dark when he saw their intended target. "My God. You're lucky you weren't killed. You must have fallen fifty feet."

"It wasn't all airborne. There was a lot of bumping and bouncing." He tried to make light of the incident, but what Patrick said was true. James, the ultimate outdoorsman, had almost ended things in his attempt to push himself to the limits. With the benefit of hindsight, he recognized how stupid he had been.

"I've got plenty of nylon rope in my pack," Patrick said. "I think the most reasonable approach will be to secure ourselves to these two trees and rappel down the incline."

"I'm game." He wasn't. Not at all. But it wasn't the physical difficulties that daunted him. He was afraid of what they were going to see.

Patrick went first. He was the more experienced when it came to this kind of task. After a few uneventful drops, he shielded his face with his hand and waved. "It's not so bad once you get over the edge. Just try to stay left so you don't kill me with a rock."

It wasn't a joke. The loose scree was mostly in little pieces, but here and there were good-sized stones, certainly big enough to damage a man's skull. Patrick landed lightly on his feet, testing the ledge for structural integrity. As James had described, it was solid.

A few moments later, James joined him. They left the ropes tied around their waists. Any unwary movement might send them tumbling, maybe not to their deaths, but certainly into danger.

"Where?" Patrick asked bluntly.

"The far end of the ledge. Where that other part sticks out and creates some shade."

He let Patrick go first, but he was right on his brother's heels. When they reached the bushes, there was enough footing for both of them to crouch hip to hip. Patrick pushed the branches aside.

There was no question that Patrick saw what James had seen. The skeleton was curiously undisturbed. Though animals might have gotten at it in the beginning, it would not have been easy to find.

Sweat rolled into James's eyes. "Reggie Kavanagh. Or what's left of him."

Patrick grunted. "Maybe. It does look old."

"It's him," James insisted. "I found this."

When Patrick saw the ring, he recoiled. "You're positive?"

"Mom's initials are in the band. And the date." James was shaking inside, but he concealed his disquiet. "What should we do now?"

"There's no way we can keep it intact."

"No." James almost felt as if an invisible spirit stood at his shoulder. Disturbing a burial ground was an offense to the dead, a sign of disrespect. He wasn't a superstitious man, but the idea of scooping up human remains and tossing them in a sack was macabre at the very least. "We should have brought gloves," he said, trying for humor.

Patrick grimaced. "At least it doesn't smell. That was gone a long time ago."

Though James had been too buzzed to think about it, Patrick had remembered to bring along several thin nylon sacks, the kind used for organizing small things in a backpack. Now the question remained, how to go about their grisly mission?

"Maybe we should take photos, like one of those CSI

shows." James was grasping at straws, anything to post-pone touching bones that carried his DNA.

"Not a bad idea at all. It might help the coroner."

"Aren't we way past a coroner? Surely this will be more of a forensic investigation."

"True." They both grabbed their phones and took sev-eral photos. The brief activity helped put some distance between them and the reality neither wanted to accept.

Finally, Patrick stared at him. "Do you want me to start?"

"I should do it. At least I don't remember him."

Patrick sighed. "I barely do. Don't laugh, but I think I'll say a prayer."

James nodded, his throat tight. "Trust me. I've never felt less like laughing."

Their mother, Maeve, was a deeply religious woman. She'd grown up listening to stories *from the homeland*, as she liked to call it, the Green Isle, the country of the leprechauns. For the Irish, it was not a good thing to mess around with the dead. They might come back to haunt you.

Patrick's steady voice broke the silence, his words borne away almost instantly on the wind. "Dear God. Bless the immortal soul of this poor, lonely creature. And if these decaying bones truly be all that is left of Reginald Kavanagh, please help James and me break the news to our family. Amen."

"Amen."

After that, there were no words at all. A child was brought up to honor a parent. This garbage expedition, for lack of a better term, seemed the rankest form of betrayal. In truth, though, the difficult and unpleasant task would help give closure to all of the Kavanaghs.

They gathered the bones one and two at a time. Patrick cradled the skull in his hands momentarily before sliding it into the sack. James saw his brother wipe his eyes and heard the shuddery sigh that reflected his sibling's grief.

They stood there for the longest time, not saying a word. Patrick's face was white, his countenance stoic.

Surprisingly, James felt almost reluctant to leave this sad, lonely ledge in the middle of nowhere. Here was the spot where his father had taken his last breath. While baby James was at home sleeping in his crib, had his father suffered? The evidence would appear to say so.

There was a pain in his chest and a tightness that wouldn't ease.

Patrick touched his arm. "We have to go."

"I know."

They tied their precious cargo to the belaying ropes and climbed side by side back up to the top. When the gear was stowed and there was no longer any reason to linger, James lifted his face to the sky and closed his eyes. For years he had harbored bitterness and resentment toward the father he had never known.

Now, in this oddly sacred moment, all of that slipped away. *I'm sorry, Dad.*

How could he be angry at a man who had spent his last hours in such a grim fashion? His father hadn't meant to die. He'd merely been reckless. Much like his youngest son.

"Look," Patrick said, his voice hushed. There above them, where the thermal currents shot up the side of the mountain and danced in the clouds, a lone hawk circled. As they watched, the bird swooped low over their heads and then disappeared behind the trees.

James's knees were weak, but his soul was light. "Let's go home."

Twenty

Lila found strength she never knew she possessed. Living meant experiencing pain. She couldn't get around it, so she would go through it. In her darkest hours, she wondered if telling James she was in love with him might have made a difference.

But it had taken her so long to see the truth, the damage was done. It was too late. She'd had a second chance. There would not be another.

Exactly a week to the day after James stormed out of Lila's life, Mia showed up at her door. She didn't have Cora with her and she hadn't called in advance. Curiouser and curiouser. "Come in," Lila said.

Mia nodded, but didn't speak. Her expression was hard to read. Was it grief? Worry? A combination of both?

Lila took her hands and pulled her toward the living room. "Sit down. You don't look well." Maybe her friend was pregnant again.

Mia perched on the edge of her seat, her hands clasped

in her lap. "James needs to see you." She stopped and corrected herself. "He *wants* to see you."

"Oh, no," Lila said. "You're mistaken. Believe me."

"Please, Lila. Give him the benefit of the doubt. He's had some hard news. You could help him, I know."

Alarm flooded her veins. "What is it? What's happened? Is he sick?" Oh, God. Was something dreadfully wrong with the man, who was as strong as an ox?

Mia's eyes were shadowed, her demeanor sober. "It's not my story to tell. He may be too proud to come here after the way you two parted, but trust me, Lila. That man is hurting. He needs you whether he wants to admit it or not. I'll stay behind and give you some privacy."

Lila went to the restroom and splashed water on her face. Her whole body was trembling. What if Mia was wrong? And did it matter? Didn't she want to help James in return for all the ways he had helped her? Even if he didn't want her *or* her help?

The walk across the side yard between her house and his had never seemed so long. She wasn't dressed to impress. Faded jeans. A thin summery top. The heat had returned just as all of Silver Glen was decorating with pumpkins and corn shocks and colorful scarecrows.

Fall was a busy time for the high-end tourist season. Last year she had seen a very famous movie star trick-or-treating with her two toddlers on Halloween night. That was still a month away. A lot could change by then.

She was dawdling. She knew it. But it was hard to get her feet to move.

At last, she knocked on the door. Maybe he wasn't home. Maybe he wouldn't hear her. But his car was in the driveway, and so was Mia's.

James opened the door almost immediately, as if he had been waiting for her. "Why aren't you at work?" he said, frowning.

"I didn't have to go in today."

He stepped back to let her enter. Then the most extraordinary thing happened. He dragged her close and buried his face in the curve of her neck. She held him tightly as faint tremors racked his body. As she stroked his hair and the back of his neck, she absorbed the heat of him, his familiar masculine scent.

Now she was really scared. Was he dying?

The not knowing was only a fraction easier than the knowing. So she held her tongue. He would tell her when he was ready.

At last he released her and wiped a hand across his face. "I need to be outside," he said. "Let's go to the backyard."

None of this made sense, but she followed him, anyway. When they reached their destination, James ignored the set of patio chairs. Instead, he led her by the hand to the wooden picnic table. They climbed up on top and sat with their feet on the bench seat.

The sun was hot on the crown of her head. Early October was always one of her favorite times of the year... summer's last hurrah before colder weather moved in for good. Soon, the smell of wood smoke would linger in the air. For Silver Glen, pleasures would abound. Mulled cider and warm sweaters. Long morning walks with your breath making white puffs when you spoke.

Even the mountain changed in this season. Its rugged contours would gradually become more visible. The green of summer would be replaced by the gray and black of a winter forest. Snow would fall.

Would she and James be civil to each other again by then? Would they go back to ignoring or avoidance?

Their hips and thighs touched. Her hands were twined in her lap. James leaned back on his hands, the handsome profile she knew so well silhouetted against the blue sky.

Her store of patience vanished. "Tell me what's going

on. Please." Terrible thoughts tormented her…could he have cancer? Or maybe something worse?

James sat up straight and stared in front of him. The line of his jaw was rigid. "I found my father's body."

The words were so low, she had to strain to hear them. "You what?"

"I found my father's body. His skeleton, to be more precise."

"Oh, James." She gaped at him. Still, he didn't look at her. "I'm so sorry." Was that even the right response? She was at a loss for words.

"I wasn't looking this time. It was an accident, a whim of fate."

"Tell me," she urged. "Tell me what happened."

In halting words and grim images, he described the sequence of events that ended with his and Patrick's heart-wrenching task. The words were dull, the cadence stilted, as if he had said it all a thousand times but still couldn't believe it was real.

When he lapsed into silence, she leaned her head against his shoulder and took one of his big hands in hers. Squeezing his fingers, she tried to telegraph her sympathy and concern.

"How is Maeve?" she finally asked.

"She's devastated. Hell, the whole family is, to one degree or another."

"How are you, James?"

He was silent for so long she thought he wasn't going to answer. Finally, he shrugged. "Empty. Sad. Ashamed."

She frowned. "Why ashamed?"

"I've spent my whole life being angry at a man who never meant to leave us. His obsession killed him, yes. But he's hardly the first or last man to lose his way."

"That's a pretty big concession from the guy I used to know. You could hardly bear to talk about him."

"I remember. I was a cocky, self-centered bastard. It was all about me. And my poor ruined childhood."

"And then I whined about mine. We're a pair, aren't we?"

His startled laugh was rusty, as if he had forgotten how. He paused. "Will you come with me to the memorial service tomorrow? It's at three. At the little wooden chapel on the town square. We'll all go up to the lodge afterward for dinner."

"Of course. I'd be honored."

He shuddered. "I haven't been sleeping."

"Nightmares?"

"Yeah."

"That sucks."

"Tell me about it."

As the minutes passed, she felt a perceptible change in James's big frame. Little by little, he relaxed. If she could do this for him, it was enough.

"Why don't you take a nap?" she said. "Maybe the dreams won't come in the daylight."

"Will you lie down with me?"

She swallowed. Mia was next door waiting. But James's sister-in-law wouldn't intrude. "If that's what you want."

In James's bedroom, she didn't know how to act. Was he asking for sex? Or something far simpler…

Fortunately, he didn't leave her guessing. He kicked off his shoes and stretched out on the bed, fully clothed. When he held out his hand, she followed suit. James spooned her back, and she felt his kiss at her nape. "Thank you," he muttered, already half asleep.

She didn't answer. How could she? Pain gripped her. They were always just a pace out of step, it seemed. Good for each other at times, but totally wrong at others. "I love you," she whispered.

He didn't answer. Of course. He was dead to the world.

She let herself stay for fifteen minutes. After that, she made herself slip out of his embrace and tiptoe out of the room.

Back at her house, Mia lifted an eyebrow. "How is he?"

"Better. He's sleeping."

Mia's eyebrows shot to her hairline. "Well, thank God. You're the only one of us who could do *that* for him."

Lila felt her face heat. "We didn't have sex, if that's what you're thinking. We only talked."

"It wouldn't have mattered if you did." Mia stood to leave. "I won't go back in his house. I don't want to disturb him. Will you fix him something for dinner? He's barely eaten since he and Patrick came off the mountain Monday afternoon."

"Of course. If he wants to eat."

"He will. Trust me. You can get through to him."

Mia left at three thirty. Lila threw together a big pot of spaghetti with meatballs. Even if James wasn't interested, she could freeze the rest.

At five, she sent a text:

I made spaghetti. Are you interested? There's plenty…

Her phone remained stubbornly silent for the next half hour. At last, a quiet ding signaled a message:

Sorry. I was in the shower. Spaghetti sounds great.

He was on her doorstep in seconds smelling like lime and evergreen and looking refreshed with damp hair and bright eyes. "Smells amazing in here," he said. "Where's Sybbie?"

"Right behind you." The baby was playing with pots and pans. Lila had turned a kitchen chair on its side and used it as a barricade across the corner to keep Sybbie from wandering. It was hard to cook with a baby under-foot...and dangerous, too.

James stood beside the stove, much too close to the chef in Lila's estimation. His gaze was sober, but his eyes danced. "You're better than a sleeping pill, woman."

"Thanks for the compliment. I love being compared to pharmaceuticals. Put some ice in the glasses, will you?"

There was a level of awkwardness in the room because of everything that had transpired in the last week, but it was mixed with an undertone of sexual awareness. She dropped a spoon and splattered hot tomato sauce all over her legs.

James grabbed a damp cloth. "Hold still. Let me get it off before you're burned."

She was wearing shorts in deference to the heat. When James put his hands on her legs, she nearly melted into a puddle of wax. "That's got it," she croaked. Looking down at the top of his head was giving her ideas.

Even James seemed rattled.

Over dinner, they chatted lightly. Sybbie was in her high chair making her presence known, so there was no question of discussing heavy topics.

After the meal, James played with the baby while Lila tidied up the kitchen. She knew the smart thing to do, but she was having a hard time following through. James needed to go to his house. If he didn't, something bad was going to happen. Or something very, very good, depend-ing on one's point of view.

She used Sybbie's drooping eyelids to shore up her re-solve. "I should get her to bed. Good night, James. I'll see you tomorrow."

"Do you know the phrase *friends with benefits*?" His expression was completely serious.

"I've heard it."

"You and I might never be good for each other in the

long term, but evidence suggests we're pretty damned phenomenal in one area. Plus, I'm pitiful and sad." He gave her a puppy dog look…which coming from a man who was six foot three and built like a rock was ludicrous.

"I always knew men would do or say anything to get sex, but playing the sympathy card is low, even for you."

The humor fled his face. "I was only teasing. About the sad part. But I've missed you, Lila. I need you tonight. Please."

It would have taken a stronger woman than she was to say no. Not when she wanted exactly what he wanted.

Twenty-One

Lila didn't give him a direct answer, though she knew what was going to happen. Even so, a brief time-out would have been nice—a chance to consider the ramifications of having sex with James Kavanagh again.

It wasn't to be. She found him underfoot during every move she made—in the bathroom bathing Sybbie, in the nursery rubbing sweet baby legs with lotion and lastly adding his deep bass accompaniment to age-old songs as the two of them sang lullabies together.

At last, her niece was asleep. "It's only seven thirty," she said. "Too early to go to bed."

"I wasn't planning on sleeping."

How could he say five small words and make her knees go weak? She held up a hand. "I don't mind you using me to get through the night. I'll enjoy that as much as you will. But I'm pretty sure that right now you need to talk more than you need to…well, you know."

He frowned. "Why do women always think talking will solve everything?"

"Because it usually does," she snorted. "If women ran the world, we'd be in a much better place. C'mon. I'll fix you some hot chocolate."

"A shot of bourbon would be more like it," he grumbled.

"It's a proven fact that alcohol disturbs your sleep. You'll like my cocoa. I put little marshmallows and real milk in it. Plus, it's Godiva. Be prepared to have your taste buds thrilled and amazed."

Given the circumstances, it seemed smarter to have their snack in the kitchen. She set out some cookies as well, but she and James were both still stuffed from dinner. With the bright overhead light, the practical ambience of appliances and the scent of lemon dishwashing liquid, it should have been easy to keep her mind off sex.

Unfortunately, she was not that strong.

Even so, she was determined to give James a chance to debrief, to share the load he was carrying. "What happened after you came back off the mountain?" she asked quietly. "How bad was it?"

He stirred his steaming beverage, following the spoon with his gaze. "Patrick and I had endless circular discussions about when and how to tell our mother. We felt she deserved to be the first to know. And besides, rounding up all the rest of the crew quickly and telling them at the same time would have been a logistical nightmare."

"So what did you do?"

"When we got back, I showered and changed into some decent clothes. Patrick did the same. He told Libby, though. The two of them have no secrets from each other, and besides, she could see he was in bad shape."

"I'm sure."

"When we were ready, or as ready as we could be, we went up the mountain together. Liam wasn't there at the moment, so it wasn't tricky to get Mom alone. We went to her office on the pretext of asking about a birthday present for one of the grandkids."

"How did you do it?"

His laugh was bitter. "There's no good way to tell someone you love a thing like that. Patrick put his arm around her. I held her hands. And I just said it."

"Poor Maeve."

"My mother is one of the strongest women I've ever met, but she aged in front of us. She crumpled. I don't know what she was thinking. Maybe she always wondered if he would simply stroll back into the room one day."

"But now she knows."

"Yeah. One good thing about having plenty of resources is that we were able to get the DNA and forensic testing done rapidly. We knew it was him, though, because we found the wedding ring. Gold lasts, you know. When we handed it to Mom, she cried like a baby. It broke my heart."

"Oh, James."

"Yeah. We don't have a definitive cause of death yet, though he did have a broken leg and a head injury. It's possible he died instantly, but it's also possible he slowly starved to death."

"You can't think about that."

"How can I not?"

Silence fell.

Lila touched his arm. "How about your brothers?"

"We called a family meeting Tuesday morning. Everyone was there in person except for Aidan. He and Emma live in New York."

"I remember."

"There was shock and…hell, I don't know. How do you grieve for someone you lost so long ago? You'd think we would have all worked through those emotions a thousand times…that we'd be done with it."

"But finding him brought it all back for the lot of you."

He sighed deeply, his head bowed. "That's what happened. Maybe this service tomorrow will help everybody move on. We won't have the actual remains for some time. We'll spread his ashes in the winter. On top of the mountain. That's where he loved to be, anyway."

"James?"

"Hmm?" He lifted his head and looked at her.

"I'm saying this in all sincerity. I think you need a decent night's sleep. You should go home."

"You don't want me here? I'll admit I'm not good company at the moment. I'll try to do better."

"Give me a break. It's not that."

His gaze was bleak. "Every time I get in bed and close my eyes, I see that skeleton all over again. A stranger's body would have been shocking. But I knew in my gut as soon as I found it, that it was Dad. I can't get it out of my head."

Suddenly, she understood. He wanted to go back in time. Sex with her was part of his past. He wasn't that young man anymore. Life and the passage of years had matured him. This terrible experience had honed him by fire. But for tonight, they could pretend.

It wasn't fair to her. She'd shed enough tears over James Kavanagh to fill a small ocean. But she couldn't say no to him. She didn't want to. If this was all they were ever going to have, it would be enough.

In the midst of his family's mutual grief, there would be no occasion for the two of them to have shouting matches or furious arguments. James was strong. But even a strong man needed help on occasion. She could be there for him. No matter the cost.

"Turn out the lights," she said quietly. "I'll grab a shower and meet you in the bedroom."

She left him in the kitchen and walked quietly down the hall, feeling both excited and despondent. Was that even possible? Maybe she was like a gambling addict about to wager everything, knowing she was going to lose it all but unable to stop herself.

That thought didn't conjure a pretty image. As she undressed and secured her hair on top of her head, she brooded. Sybbie and James. Two puzzles with no discernible correct answers. All she could do was keep trying until she found the right path.

After adjusting the water and waiting for it to warm up, she opened the transparent fiberglass door and stepped into the shower enclosure.

"I'll help wash your back."

The deep voice startled her so badly she nearly lost her balance.

"James?"

He stripped off his pants. "Who did you think it was?"

Her bathroom had always seemed ample in size, particularly for such an old house. But when James moved next to her, the walls closed in. He was big and tanned all over except for a wide strip around his hip. He was also manly in just the right way. The fine hair on his arms and legs and torso was light brown scattered with a smattering of red-gold.

He reminded her of a Norse god.

She refused to look any lower than his rib cage. It was hard enough to breathe as it was. "You take a lot for granted," she said, backing up until her butt was plastered against the wall.

"We've showered together before."

But not for a very long time. Back then they had been playful and spontaneous and carefree. Then came the quarrels. And now, three years later, life had turned pretty damned serious for both of them.

She turned her back to him. "If you're here, you might as well make yourself useful."

* * *

James took the shower gel and the washcloth and worked up a sudsy lather. He was going to smell like apples when this was all over, but there were worse things. Lila stood perfectly still, the line from her neck to the bottom of her spine pure poetry.

He was breaking his own personal code. He was taking advantage of a woman. With her consent, but still. Lila was too decent to turn him away. God help him, he was thankful for her generous heart.

Being in his house alone gave him too much time to think. He could stay with one of his married brothers… or up at the hotel for a few nights. But he didn't want to admit to any of them how much this whole experience had traumatized him. Though he didn't know it until this past weekend on the mountain, at some level he had convinced himself his father hadn't really died out in the woods. With no body discovered, he had come to believe that the old man might show up one day and want to connect with the son he never really knew.

The subconscious was a devious bastard. Seeing irrefutable proof of his father's demise crushed those unlikely dreams. He'd known intellectually that his father was never coming back. Now his gut knew it, too.

Shaking off the unpleasant thoughts that plagued him, he concentrated on pleasing Lila. Washing her back was both tame and sweet. He palmed her butt cheeks and swished the cloth in between.

Lila jumped three inches. "That's enough," she said.

"Spoilsport." He turned her around and sucked in a breath, feeling as if someone had smacked him with a board. He knew what she looked like. He had seen her naked again and again. But tonight, all wet and soapy and warm, she was incredible.

With her full breasts and rounded hips, Lila's waist

seemed impossibly small. He settled his hands there to keep them out of trouble.

Lila looked down, surely unable to miss the way his erection bobbed eagerly. "You dropped the washcloth," she whispered. Her eyes were huge. She stared at him as if fascinated. It was a two-way street.

"Kiss me," he muttered. "Before I go insane." One small nod broke the leash he'd kept on his self-control. He dragged her close, shoving his mouth over hers, ravaging her soft lips with his rough kisses.

The taste of her filled his brain. It was chocolate and apples and sex all in one heady cocktail. Lila arched against him, her arms locked around his neck. The feel of her breasts smashed up against his chest made him dizzy. He wanted her. But his brain was so befuddled, he wasn't able to think past this moment. He knew he had to make it from the shower to her bed, but he couldn't let go. He wouldn't.

Lila put her leg around his hip, trying to get closer. She was slick and wet. It was all he could do to keep them both upright.

At last she took mercy on him. "James."

He bit her earlobe. "Hmm?"

Lila groaned. "I'm getting out now. To dry off."

He put his hands underneath her thighs and lifted her into his pelvis, grinding his swollen sex against the vee of her legs. "Not yet," he begged. "Not yet."

With the water raining down on both of them, he put her back on her feet and sank to his knees, kissing his way from her navel to her feminine secrets.

He probed gently, first with his thumb and then the tip of his tongue. Lila cried out and collapsed in his arms.

Somehow he managed to turn off the water and get both of them out of the shower. "Hold still, love. Let me dry you."

He ran the soft towel all over her, pausing to kiss favorite spots along the way. Her eyelids were heavy, her lips puffy and swollen from his kisses. He scooped her into his arms and carried her to the bedroom. Instead of checking the monitor, they both peeked in on Sybbie. The baby slept peacefully.

Lila's head lolled against his shoulder. "Tell me what you want, James."

He laid her with gentle reverence on the mattress and reached for a condom. When that was taken care of, he moved over her and into her. He kissed her eyelids one at a time. "I have everything I want," he swore. "Everything."

Lila sensed the desperation in his lovemaking. Was it for her, or was he immersing himself in sex so he wouldn't think…wouldn't feel?

He was a large man. All over. The way he claimed her so aggressively tapped into something primitive in her pleasure centers. Her body opened for him…stretched to accommodate him. When he moved carefully, in and out, she climbed again, her body eager for the release he gave her every time.

And at the end when he thrust wildly—out of control—she relished the bruises she might find on her wrists the next day. Because having James in her bed and being dragged headlong into the fire with him was the deepest pleasure she had ever known.

Twenty-Two

When she awoke Saturday morning, James was gone. She was neither surprised nor hurt. She had vague, drowsy memories of him kissing her forehead and whispering goodbye as the first faint light of dawn spilled into her bedroom.

The pillow on which he'd slept still carried his scent. She hugged it to her chest, telling herself her eyes weren't damp. This day would be a difficult one for all the Kavanaghs. James would need to have his head in the game to make it through unscathed.

At nine o'clock she received an unusually lengthy text from Mia:

Dylan hasn't been able to get in touch with James, so we're assuming he's with you. I'm supposed to let you know the family has arranged for child care at a home near the chapel. I made sure Sybbie was included in the count. The three high school babysitters are super-dependable. I'm leaving Cora with them, and you know

how picky I am. J We'll swing by and let you follow us. Is
two o'clock too early? Dylan wants to be there to greet
people...

Lila answered the text with one hand while feeding Sybbie. The little girl was still at the age to be open and happy
with strangers, so hopefully, this would work. Deciding
what to wear was another issue. Most of Lila's clothes were
either professional business attire or supercasual.

She did have one black dress, but it was a little sexy for
a funeral. While Sybbie played on the floor of the closet
with blocks, Lila slipped into the dress and looked in the
mirror on the back of the door. The length wasn't a problem. The hemline hit right at her knees. Even in heels it
would be modest.

But the crossover-wrap bodice was another story. The
dress was a bit retro—1940s maybe. She'd seen it in a de-
partment store window last Christmas and fallen in love
with it, though she had never had a chance to wear it. The
waist was fitted, the skirt flared. Tiny cap sleeves bared
most of her arms. It was the plunging neckline she worried about. Her D-cup breasts weren't going to hide in
this little number. Maybe with the judicious placement of
a safety pin, it would work.

After combing through the rest of her closet, she decided it was the black dress or nothing. She really didn't
want to wear a tailored business suit, and everything else
she had leaned toward shoulder-baring sundresses. Silver
Glen might be having a warm spell, but she couldn't show
up looking as if she were on her way to a picnic.

Besides, it was the only black dress she owned. Not everyone stuck to that black rule anymore. The Kavanaghs
were like local royalty in Silver Glen, though. Lila wanted
to look nice for James, even if the occasion was a som-
ber one.

As it turned out, she made the right choice. Mia turned up wearing a simple little black dress, and Dylan was in a black suit that was clearly not off the rack. It fit him perfectly.

When the three of them arrived at the church after dropping off the two little girls, most of the family had gathered. As Lila had suspected, they were all in formal black. This must be what a Kennedy funeral looked like, she thought, bemused by the sight of so many Kavanaghs in one room.

She lingered at the back of the small frame church. The warm, unfinished wood and clear glass windows hearkened back to a simpler time. Though the pews could seat only eighty or so, the town had erected a tent just outside with a large screen and a live feed.

Only Maeve's contemporaries would remember Reggie Kavanagh. The family as a whole, however, was well liked and well respected. Their many friends and acquaintances would turn out in droves to pay their respects.

The church filled up rapidly, but not before Lila had refreshed her memory about the Kavanagh family tree. Liam, the eldest, was there with Zoe. Then came Dylan and Mia, of course. They were the only two family members Lila knew well.

Third in line was the financial genius Aidan and his English wife, Emma. In the middle was Gavin, whose spouse was the bubbly Cassidy. Conor had married his childhood friend Ellie, who was at his side today. Rounding out the group, except for James, was Patrick, who had shared the ordeal of recovering what was left of the senior Kavanagh. Patrick's wife, Libby, was the newest member of the tight-knit clan.

Lila perched on the last pew at the end of a row. There were probably a few people she knew here today. After all, it was a small town. But she chose to sit alone and absorb the timeless comfort of this unassuming house of worship that dated back to the early days of Silver Glen.

Without warning, an official-looking man from the funeral home tapped her on the shoulder. "Excuse me, ma'am. Are you Lila Baxter?"

She nodded slowly.

"The family has asked that you sit up front with them."

"Oh, no," Lila said. "I'm not related."

"Mr. Kavanagh insisted," he said. "Mr. James Kavanagh," the man clarified, as if realizing his mistake.

With the obsequious employee waiting patiently, she had to stand up and go with him, or make an uncomfortable scene.

So she went.

She wasn't worried about the eyes that followed her progress to the front of the church. But she was definitely flustered when most of James's family greeted her quietly with brief smiles of welcome. James sat on his mother's left, Patrick on her right. One empty spot had been saved on James's left. Apparently, it had Lila's name on it.

Thankfully, it was time for the service to start. The piano music swelled and floated up to the rafters. James reached for her hand and clasped it in his. The remainder of the Kavanagh clan sat to the right and left and behind Maeve.

There were no fancy accoutrements. Two candles burned on the altar. Two arrangements of white lilies flanked the lectern. A minister friend of the family read Scripture and had a prayer. Then Liam stood up to give the eulogy. Lila didn't envy him his task.

A few seconds elapsed before he uttered the first word. She had an idea he was gathering himself *and* his thoughts. At last, he began...

"My father was a man like any other man, with good traits and bad. I was old enough to grieve his passing and understand what it meant. But I was still a boy. I tried my best to fill my father's shoes, but it was our mother, Maeve, who held this family together and made us all believe our world would be okay."

He stopped and blew a kiss to his mom. The sweet moment lightened some of the tension in the room. Then he continued.

"Reginald Kavanagh, or Reggie as you might have known him, was fascinated with the story of the silver mine that launched the family fortunes and made the town of Silver Glen a reality. Our ancestors fled lives of poverty and hard times across the ocean to come to an unfamiliar country and start anew.

"Over the decades that followed, the mine was tapped out, I'm sure. The actual location was lost. Grown over. Filled in. No one really knows. But my father couldn't let that go. He wanted to find the mine, wanted it more than was healthy. And now we know he lost his life in that quest."

When Liam paused, there was a bit of uneasy rustling in the room. As eulogies went, this one was unusually frank. He grimaced. "You might wonder why I'm telling you this. After all, many of you know the story as well as I do. It's the stuff of legend, I suppose. But in this small chapel, as we remember and say goodbye to my father, I want to challenge each of you to take stock of what's important in life.

"It's easy to get off track. Believe me, I know. Life crowds in. Responsibilities. Worries. But look around you. We share this town and this dream of a place where the air is clean and the mountains are ancient and the water flows sparkling in the sun. Don't let life pass you by. Don't chase after things that don't matter.

"We grieve again for Reggie Kavanagh, here and now. He loved my mother. He loved his sons. And he loved this

quiet valley. My family and I are so grateful for your presence today. It means more than you know. As we all step
forth into the sunshine in a few moments, lift up your eyes
to the hills. Listen to the wind. Watch the clouds scurry
across the sky. And if you will, say a prayer for my father
and his immortal soul. His end was inglorious, but we
loved him. We love him still. Thank you."

Lila had no tissues in her small black clutch. That was
a rookie mistake. Liam's eloquent words struck a chord in
her that had nothing to do with Reggie Kavanagh at all.

As the closing music played softly, James reached in his
pocket and handed her a white cotton handkerchief. "Don't
be such a girl," he whispered. His attempt at humor wasn't
helpful. His lopsided grin made her heart hurt even more.

Friends crowded in to speak to the family. Lila seized
the opportunity to sneak away. She had been invited to
the dinner afterward up at the Silver Beeches Lodge, but
she couldn't bear it. She wasn't part of this wonderful,
grieving family. She had Sybbie to think about, though
she wouldn't be rude.

She paused on the sidewalk outside the church and sent
James a text: I don't feel comfortable intruding on your
family's private time. I'm glad I could be there for the
service.

After hitting Send, she almost had second thoughts.
But she was doing the right thing. There was no need for
people to get the misguided idea that she and James were
a couple again. It was a good bet that most of his family
remembered the fireworks the last time. And not the good
kind of fireworks.

In some ways, she wished she could be the biddable,
traditional woman James wanted and needed. That kind of
female would fit right in with the amazing Kavanaghs…
wearing pearls to vacuum the carpet, preparing a three-

course meal every evening, throwing dinner parties for fifty without blinking an eye.

Maybe if Sybbie hadn't come into her life, Lila and James could have tried again. As she paid her share of the babysitting fee and thanked the three young women who were caring for the children, she knew she had to tell James her decision about her niece. But later, not today when he had so much on his plate.

She hadn't been able to go grocery shopping in the last few days, so there was not much back at the house in the way of dinner. Since the late-afternoon sun was warm, and because Sybbie enjoyed being in the car, Lila decided to pick up a few things at the small market near the church. Fresh-baked bread. Grapes. Cheddar cheese. Some baby food as well, in case Sybbie didn't appreciate the gourmet fare.

They drove away from town, mile after mile, toward the end of the valley where the mountains came together again and the road turned into a narrow gravel lane. She found a handy pull-off and went around to the backseat. "Here you go, my love. This is a splendid place for a picnic."

The novelty of the situation seemed to perplex Sybbie, though she ate without fussing. Afterward, Lila took her out of the car seat and held her hands as she toddled around trying to assert her independence. It wouldn't be long. She'd be walking before Christmas.

Shadows fell as the light faded. A chill filled the air. Lila pondered her decision and hoped she was doing the right thing. Monday morning she and Sybbie would go to Asheville and see what arrangements could be made. As Liam reminded everyone, Lila had to keep her eye on what was important.

It was past the baby's bedtime when they got back home. Lila didn't bother changing clothes. She kicked off her heels and carried the drowsy infant into the new nursery. Bath time could wait until tomorrow. A clean diaper, fresh jammies, and soon the little one was sucking her fist as she liked to do.

Lila sat down in the rocking chair and cuddled her niece. Sybbie was a warm, sweet weight against her breasts. She'd never thought much about actually being pregnant. Her formative years had been too rocky for her to entertain Norman Rockwell fantasies about nesting and other maternal prerogatives.

Now, though, she began to see the pull. A baby was a blessing and a joy. Not easy. Certainly not easy. But she understood why men and woman kept repeating the process.

At last, reluctantly, she laid the baby in her bed. When she turned to tiptoe out of the room, she stepped back, startled, her heart racing. James stood framed in the doorway. He still wore his dark suit, though his tie was loose at the throat and the two top buttons of his shirt were unfastened.

In the dim light he looked tired and grim and utterly wonderful. "You scared me to death," she whispered. "How did you get in here?"

"I still have a key." He held out his hand. "You never asked for it back."

He might have been talking about the last couple of weeks and the renovation, but it was more than that. For the past three years, they had each kept a key to the other's house. What did that mean?

Though their conversation was reduced to low-voiced whispers, neither of them made a move to leave the room. Maybe they both realized it was safer that way. With Sybbie as a chaperone, they had to behave.

She wrapped her arms around her waist and leaned against the end of the crib. "Why are you here? You should be with your family."

He shrugged. "Everyone went home soon after dinner.

The kids needed their beds and the adults were headed for an early night, too. Today was brutal."

"I know. But the service was beautiful. I hope your mother was pleased."

"I think so. She's seemed so damned frail these last few days it's scaring us to death. Patrick and Libby took her home with them tonight so she wouldn't have to be alone."

"Probably a good idea."

"I don't know if you heard, but my date dumped me at my own father's funeral."

"I wasn't your date. And I didn't dump you. I merely skipped the family dinner. I'm not family."

He glared. "And you're doing your best to keep it that way, aren't you?"

Twenty-Three

She gaped at him, her temper mounting. "What does that mean?" she whispered. "I know you've had a rough day, but I'm not in the mood to go three rounds with you tonight. If you have something to say, spit it out."

He scraped his hands through his hair, making it stand up on end. "Can we please get out of this room where I can actually talk to you?"

"Whatever you want." The words were nice, but unfortunately, her tone was not. She didn't need to see James. Not like this. Life needed to move on. Breathing the same air he breathed hurt too much.

She had no choice but to follow as he left the baby's quiet sanctuary. Otherwise, she wouldn't put it past him to camp out until she let him have his say. They ended up in the living room. Sybbie's toys were scattered across the rug. Lila had barely had time to think today, much less tidy up.

Plucking a baby doll out of a chair, she sank into the soft cushions, closed her eyes and rested her head on the back. "Why are you here, James? What do you want?"

She had left the sofa for him, but James didn't sit. Instead, he paced, his expression aggrieved. "I want to talk about why you ran out of the funeral."

"I don't think tonight is the time or place for a serious discussion. You've had a very difficult day. We're both tired. We need to relax."

"What are you suggesting?" He stared at her with suspicion.

In his shoes, she'd be suspicious, too. "You're here. I'm here. We might as well enjoy it."

His face turned red. "You wouldn't jerk me around after the day I've had…surely you wouldn't."

She held out a hand. "Come with me, Mr. Kavanagh. I'll make that headache go away."

"How do you know I have a headache?"

His scowl did nothing to deter her. He was hurting. Emotionally. Physically. She might not have the typical maternal instincts, but she could fix this. "I know you," she said softly. "Warts and all."

He didn't refute her claim. Instead, he made sure the front door was locked, and he turned out the lights. She waited for him in the hallway. When he finally took her hand with a grumpy mumble that signified nothing, she hid a smile.

In the bedroom, she lit a candle. "Do you like my dress?" she asked artfully.

"A little too much. Though in all fairness, it *did* help me get through Liam's wordy speech."

She unfastened her hair and combed her fingers through it. "I thought his eulogy was eloquent and lovely."

As he shrugged out of his jacket and unbuttoned his shirt, he stared at her with an expression she couldn't fathom. "I think a change of subject is in order. Funerals and sex don't mix."

"That's not exactly true. Psychologists say that facing

death makes people want to affirm life." She waved a hand at the bed. "I can't think of a better way."

"Maybe so." He stepped out of his trousers and tossed them on a chair. Now he wore only a pair of black knit boxers. "I'd rather talk about how your breasts nearly popped out of that thing."

"They didn't," she protested indignantly. "I used double-sided tape."

"You're kidding…" His incredulous look questioned her intellect.

"It's a time-honored trick on the red carpet. Can we please stop talking about my boobs? I'm supposed to be cheering you up."

His lazy grin sent a tingle down her spine. "Boobs are cheerful. Ask any man." He inhaled sharply. "Do you need help with that dress? As nice as it is, I'd rather have you naked."

"You could unzip me." She turned her back to him and waited.

When his slightly rough fingertips brushed her nape, she made a sound that was not quite a moan, but embarrassingly close.

James lowered the zipper one vertebrae at a time. When he got to the bottom of the line, he discovered her naughty undies. "Holy hell. How come I've never seen these before?"

She whirled to face him, holding the dress to her chest. "They're new. I decided to branch out. White cotton is so boring."

James tugged the dress from her death grip, grinning broadly when she winced. The tape left marks on her skin. "Poor baby," he said. He kissed each reddened rectangle… which led to some nipple play…which led to both of them being stark naked and pressed up against each other with dizzying effect.

"I'm sorry about your father, James," she whispered. She took his face in her hands, feeling the rough evidence of late-day stubble. "I'm sorry you had to be the one to find him. But more than that, I'm sorry I didn't understand all those times you went out on the mountain looking for him. I didn't know how much it meant to you."

"It's over now."

"Yes." She searched his face, looking for answers to questions she couldn't quite verbalize. "He would have been so very proud of you."

James took one of her hands and curled the fingers into her palm, kissing them gently. "I like to think so. My mother told me once that he loved to build things with his own two hands...even when they had the money to buy what they needed. I have his tools, you know. She gave them to me when I was sixteen."

"That's sweet."

"I was an ass. I've never taken them out of the box. It was my way of getting back at him. Stupid, isn't it? That I let a dead man have so much control over my life."

"Stupid, maybe, but understandable."

"I'm not going to be that sullen kid anymore. Reggie Kavanagh's blood flows in my veins. I can't escape it. So I might as well embrace it. He was a good storyteller, you know. There's many an old man in Silver Glen who remembers sitting down at the pub on a Saturday night listening to my father spin a yarn."

"Your mother wouldn't have fallen in love with him if he hadn't been a charmer. And if he was a fraction as handsome as any one of his seven sons, he must have had women crawling all over him."

"As a teenager, yes. But when he laid eyes on my mom, that was it. He was faithful to her for the rest of his life. That was quite a feat, because Reggie loved the ladies."

"You have your mother's integrity and work ethic. But I think that naughty gleam in your eyes must be from him."

James picked her up and carried her the two feet to the bed. "No more talking," he said huskily. "Thinking of you like this was the only thing that got me through this interminable day."

He joined her under the covers, slipped on a condom, pushed inside her and linked his hands with hers, holding her arms over her head. Bowing, he rested his forehead against hers. "Don't move for the next eight hours," he said. "I'll be okay now."

She wanted to play with his hair, but then again, this position was titillating. "My poor James. Does the big brawny man need me for a pillow?"

"Not a pillow." He flexed his hips. "More like a comforter. On a cold winter night."

Stunned, she closed her eyes and focused on the feel of him deep inside her. When had the gentle giant become a poet?

Afterward, she couldn't remember how long they moved and strained together, limbs twined, lips hungry and impatient...dueling. Begging. If she never let him go, that would be too soon.

Pain beckoned just offstage...the reality of their situation and the inevitable arguments they never seemed to get past. She pushed everything away. Tonight was for James. If she stole her share of happiness as well, what could it hurt?

She wanted it to last forever. It didn't. Like mist vanishing above a lake in the early morning sunshine, release swept through her and winnowed away. Sweeter this time, less wild.

James came after she did, his muffled groan against the curve of her neck echoing in her heart.

At last, he rolled off her. With an arm slung over his

forehead, he looked like a big hungry lion, momentarily sated, but ready to pounce at the next opportunity. Though he scarcely moved, one hand played lazily with her hair. Her earlobes were actually erogenous zones when James was in her bed.

When she had caught her breath, she lifted up on one elbow. The great slugging beats of her heart couldn't be blamed on the gratifying orgasm. She was scared. Really scared. But she clung to the words that had echoed in the small chapel. *Remember what's important.*

Suddenly James turned on his side to face her. "Maybe this is not the time, but I want to talk to you about Sybbie."

Her heart sank in the midst of disappointment that he would ruin this rare moment when they were in perfect accord. "Sybbie?" She swallowed, her throat tight with tears. She hated feeling so vulnerable. And maybe, just maybe, she was disappointed that he wanted to talk about her niece and not the two of them. "You can't let it go, can you? You can't fathom the fact that I might actually make smart, healthy decisions for my own family. You always have to be right. You always have to get the final word. Well, news flash, Mr. High-and-Mighty-Kavanagh. I'm a grown woman."

Despite every resolution to the contrary, she was arguing with him. Again.

He was pale, his gaze haunted. "You've already made a decision, haven't you? Even though I begged you to give it two months."

"This has nothing to do with you," she insisted. "And yes. I *have* made a decision. Sybbie and I are going to Asheville on Monday to make some arrangements."

James's entire demeanor changed. He sat up in bed, his back against the headboard, the sheet pulled to his waist, his expression stony. She did the same, but she grabbed the woolen coverlet at the foot of the bed and wrapped up in it, her heart bruised. Liam's words kept coming back to her. What was the answer? What was she supposed to do?

After a long, painful silence, James reached across the no-man's land that separated them and took her hand. His expression stunned her. All the barriers were down, all the hostility gone. "Don't do it, Lila. Please. I'm begging you. I wish I could have it all—you, Sybbie, us as a family. But I don't think that's in the cards. So let *me* adopt Sybbie. Please. That way she'll still be close by so you can spend time with her when your work schedule allows. I'm crazy about that little girl already. You can't send her away. Please tell me you won't."

She stared at him, transfixed. There was something he wasn't saying. Something he was hiding. But why? "Nobody lets single men adopt infants."

"You'd be surprised. Besides, if it *takes a village* to rear a child, I've got that covered right here in Silver Glen, a whole passel of Kavanaghs eager to help out."

"You've talked to them about Sybbie? Sybbie and you?"

"No. But I know my family. I wouldn't be doing this alone."

"Ah. And you're rich, isn't that the bottom line? You think all those millions you have in the bank give you the right to take my baby away from me."

"Oh, for God's sake. I'm not *taking* her. You'd be giving her to me."

She lifted her chin. "Over my dead body. How do I know you're a fit parent? What about home visits and questionnaires and health checks?" Fear made her reckless.

His eyes flashed. Shooting to his feet, he strode to the other side of the room, buck naked, maybe to keep from strangling her. "I live right next door, Lila. You'd have a bird's-eye view of my parenting skills."

Lila needed time to think. This was too pivotal a moment to screw things up. "I'm thirsty," she said. "And my feet hurt. Will you bring me a Coke?"

She thought he might protest. He was in the middle of a James-sized snit, and here she was, poking the savage beast.

When he left, she assessed the situation. Even during James's impassioned plea to adopt Sybbie, he hadn't been able to keep his eyes off Lila's cleavage. And though he still wasn't thrilled about her job, at least he was trying to understand.

When he returned with her drink, an icy glass of cola that soothed her parched throat, she sipped it slowly, staring at him over the rim. He sat down beside her. She licked her lips and cleared her throat. "I will consider letting you adopt Sybbie under one condition."

James narrowed his eyes. "And what might that be?"

She gambled big…one rash, all-in roll of the dice. "You have to take me, too."

James went perfectly still. Was he even breathing?

"You want me to adopt you?" he asked. His voice sounded funny. As if he had swallowed a bite of food the wrong way.

"No." She sat up, not bothering with the sheet for modesty. He'd seen it all, anyway. "I want you to marry me."

The grin began like a tiny smirk and spread across his face until his eyes glittered with amusement. "Why would I do that, Lila?" he asked softly.

She was trembling so hard her teeth hurt. "Because you love me." She stopped, a huge pain in her chest. "You do love me…don't you?"

He grabbed the glass and put it aside. Then he wrapped his arms around her and hugged her so tightly her ribs threatened to crack. "Of course I do, you maddening woman. And it's about damn time you proposed."

Her jaw dropped. She pulled back to stare into his golden eyes. "I don't understand."

"It's simple, my stubborn love. We've spent the whole of our relationship jockeying for position, both of us wanting to be in charge, both of us trying to call the shots. When you came across my side yard with a baby on your hip and asked for my help, it was my chance to finally get it right, though I sure as hell didn't see it that way at first."

"What changed your mind?"

"Watching you with Sybbie. I began to realize that if you could love her so much when you only just met her, that maybe you and I had a chance after all, despite our past."

"We're the same people we were back then." It was a thought that haunted her even now.

"True. But we're older and wiser. I still want to jump your bones every time you walk past me, but I've mellowed. I may not ever understand why that boring bank job means so much to you, but I'm trying. You've worked long and hard, and you deserve to have the career you want. My work is flexible. We'll find a good nanny. We'll make it happen, Lila. No matter what it takes."

"Um, about that," she muttered.

He blanched. "Surely you haven't already signed the adoption papers. You told me you and Sybbie were going to Asheville on Monday."

"We are," she said, the tears in her eyes happy ones. "We're going to see what I have to do to be a certified tax preparer in the state of North Carolina. It's work I can do from home, and it will keep my skills sharp when the babies are growing up."

"How many babies?" He eased her onto her back and stroked her flat stomach, his expression arrested.

She sucked in a sharp breath, feeling dizzy and elated. "You're going to have to renovate a big house. We may want four or five. You're the competitive one. I assumed we'd have to keep up with your brothers."

Leaning over her on one elbow, he kissed her sweetly. "We will never argue in front of our kids."

"Agreed." She nipped his bottom lip with sharp teeth. "And you'll only tell me what to do when it comes to auto mechanics, outdoor skills and carpentry."

"When you're bossy, I get to spank you."

"I don't think you understand how negotiation works."

James rolled onto his back, settling her on top of him. "I play to win. As long as you remember that, we'll be fine."

She curled up on his chest, feeling drowsy and grateful and quietly jubilant. "Well, I'm ahead on that score already, because everything I ever wanted is right here in this house. I love you, James Kavanagh. To infinity and beyond."

His deep chuckle rumbled through her. "Game, set, match. There's no one I'd rather battle. As long as all of our fights end up like this."

"I promise," she whispered, her eyelids heavy. "I promise."

Twenty-Four

"I'm *not* wearing a pink cummerbund and vest," James roared. "I look ridiculous."

"It was *your* idea to get married on Valentine's Day. Maybe you were trying to save money on future anniversaries. Don't think you can slide by with candy and flowers every year, James Kavanagh. I expect to be suitably impressed. Now put on the damn tux and quit complaining."

"If you're so suspicious of my motives, maybe we should call the whole thing off."

Now that she took a closer look, he was wild-eyed and a little green around the gills. "Oh, my gosh. You're scared, aren't you?" she said. "Scared to walk down an itty-bitty aisle and say a few simple vows in front of God and your family."

"Don't forget the whole freaking town," he muttered. He put two fingers beneath his Pepto-Bismol-pink bow tie and tugged impatiently. "Seriously. We don't have to get married today. We could wait until June. Or October. Maybe a nice Christmassy ceremony."

She lifted her chin, her frown fierce. "It's today or not at all. I won't budge on this one. You're being completely irrational."

Crossing the room in two loping strides, he took her shoulders in his hands and got up in her face. Her wedding gown was a gorgeous affair of ivory lace and satin. Sybbie would be wearing a tiny matching version.

James's big hands were warm on her bare shoulders. "Why?" he asked desperately. "Why today? We could tell them I have food poisoning. That way we can keep the gifts."

She tapped her foot, one of two clad in soft, feminine ballet slippers. "Today, James. Suck it up and be a man. If you want me, today's the day."

"But why?" he shouted. "Why do you have to be so damned stubborn?"

Without warning, she leaned into him, inhaling the comforting smell of his aftershave mixed with starched cotton. "Because I'm pregnant, you big goof. And in another week, this beautiful dress won't come close to fitting me. So there."

James staggered backward, releasing her abruptly and falling into a chair. "Pregnant? But we already have a baby. She had her first birthday party four weeks ago. I was there."

Lila shrugged, looking at him mulishly. Her bottom lip trembled. "I don't know what to tell you. They'll be close together. I'm scared, James."

He lurched to his feet and scooped her up, yards of sexy fabric cascading over his arms. "Don't cry, darlin'. Everything's going to be okay. I'm a beast. You were right about that. But I'll make it up to you somehow."

"You swear?"

He kissed her softly, feeling his chest squeeze with a

love so deep he could hardly bear it. "I swear, Lila. Anything."

"Lean down so I can whisper it in your ear," she said.

His pulse raced. "I like the sound of that."

Her gentle lips brushed his earlobe. A sweet feminine breath caressed his cheek. "Put on the vest and cummerbund, Mr. Kavanagh," she said softly. "And let's go get married."

* * * * *

*If you liked this tale of romance and family,
pick up these other stories from
USA TODAY bestselling author
Janice Maynard:*

*THE SECRET CHILD & THE COWBOY CEO
THE BILLIONAIRE'S BORROWED BABY
A BILLIONAIRE FOR CHRISTMAS
BABY FOR KEEPS
TWINS ON THE WAY*

Available now from Harlequin Desire!

***

*And don't miss the next
BILLIONAIRES AND BABIES story
THE BOSS'S BABY ARRANGEMENT
by USA TODAY bestselling author Catherine Mann.
Available September 2016!*

***

*If you're on Twitter, tell us what you think
of Harlequin Desire! #harlequindesire*

MILLS & BOON®
Hardback – August 2016

ROMANCE

The Di Sione Secret Baby	Maya Blake
Carides's Forgotten Wife	Maisey Yates
The Playboy's Ruthless Pursuit	Miranda Lee
His Mistress for a Week	Melanie Milburne
Crowned for the Prince's Heir	Sharon Kendrick
In the Sheikh's Service	Susan Stephens
Marrying Her Royal Enemy	Jennifer Hayward
Claiming His Wedding Night	Louise Fuller
An Unlikely Bride for the Billionaire	Michelle Douglas
Falling for the Secret Millionaire	Kate Hardy
The Forbidden Prince	Alison Roberts
The Best Man's Guarded Heart	Katrina Cudmore
Seduced by the Sheikh Surgeon	Carol Marinelli
Challenging the Doctor Sheikh	Amalie Berlin
The Doctor She Always Dreamed Of	Wendy S. Marcus
The Nurse's Newborn Gift	Wendy S. Marcus
Tempting Nashville's Celebrity Doc	Amy Ruttan
Dr White's Baby Wish	Sue MacKay
For Baby's Sake	Janice Maynard
An Heir for the Billionaire	Kat Cantrell

MILLS & BOON®
Large Print – August 2016

ROMANCE

The Sicilian's Stolen Son	Lynne Graham
Seduced into Her Boss's Service	Cathy Williams
The Billionaire's Defiant Acquisition	Sharon Kendrick
One Night to Wedding Vows	Kim Lawrence
Engaged to Her Ravensdale Enemy	Melanie Milburne
A Diamond Deal with the Greek	Maya Blake
Inherited by Ferranti	Kate Hewitt
The Billionaire's Baby Swap	Rebecca Winters
The Wedding Planner's Big Day	Cara Colter
Holiday with the Best Man	Kate Hardy
Tempted by Her Tycoon Boss	Jennie Adams

HISTORICAL

The Widow and the Sheikh	Marguerite Kaye
Return of the Runaway	Sarah Mallory
Saved by Scandal's Heir	Janice Preston
Forbidden Nights with the Viscount	Julia Justiss
Bound by One Scandalous Night	Diane Gaston

MEDICAL

His Shock Valentine's Proposal	Amy Ruttan
Craving Her Ex-Army Doc	Amy Ruttan
The Man She Could Never Forget	Meredith Webber
The Nurse Who Stole His Heart	Alison Roberts
Her Holiday Miracle	Joanna Neil
Discovering Dr Riley	Annie Claydon

MILLS & BOON®
Hardback – September 2016

ROMANCE

To Blackmail a Di Sione	Rachael Thomas
A Ring for Vincenzo's Heir	Jennie Lucas
Demetriou Demands His Child	Kate Hewitt
Trapped by Vialli's Vows	Chantelle Shaw
The Sheikh's Baby Scandal	Carol Marinelli
Defying the Billionaire's Command	Michelle Conder
The Secret Beneath the Veil	Dani Collins
The Mistress That Tamed De Santis	Natalie Anderson
Stepping into the Prince's World	Marion Lennox
Unveiling the Bridesmaid	Jessica Gilmore
The CEO's Surprise Family	Teresa Carpenter
The Billionaire from Her Past	Leah Ashton
A Daddy for Her Daughter	Tina Beckett
Reunited with His Runaway Bride	Robin Gianna
Rescued by Dr Rafe	Annie Claydon
Saved by the Single Dad	Annie Claydon
Sizzling Nights with Dr Off-Limits	Janice Lynn
Seven Nights with Her Ex	Louisa Heaton
The Boss's Baby Arrangement	Catherine Mann
Billionaire Boss, M.D.	Olivia Gates

0816 GEN STD HB

MILLS & BOON®
Large Print – September 2016

ROMANCE

HISTORICAL

MEDICAL

MILLS & BOON®

Why shop at millsandboon.co.uk?

Each year, thousands of romance readers find their perfect read at millsandboon.co.uk. That's because we're passionate about bringing you the very best romantic fiction. Here are some of the advantages of shopping at www.millsandboon.co.uk:

* **Get new books first**—you'll be able to buy your favourite books one month before they hit the shops

* **Get exclusive discounts**—you'll also be able to buy our specially created monthly collections, with up to 50% off the RRP

* **Find your favourite authors**—latest news, interviews and new releases for all your favourite authors and series on our website, plus ideas for what to try next

* **Join in**—once you've bought your favourite books, don't forget to register with us to rate, review and join in the discussions

Visit **www.millsandboon.co.uk**
for all this and more today!